VOLUME

The Sign of the Skull

Killer looked at his gun and almost swallowed his cigar. The skull mark was on the barrel of his shining automatic. He rubbed at it weakly and for a moment was speechless. He remembered as he crouched under the table, the gun held out, something had brushed by, something as light as a butterfly. Was that it? Had it been that close? Close enough to kill him in the dark? He rubbed at the mark on the gun. Whatever it was, it wouldn't rub off.

Hermes Press

Published by Hermes Press, an imprint of Herman and Geer Communications, Inc.
Daniel Herman, Publisher
Louise Geer, Vice President
Troy Musguire, Production Manager
Eileen Sabrina Herman, Managing Editor
Alissa Fisher, Graphic Design
Kandice Hartner, Archivist and Graphic Design
2100 Wilmington Road
Neshannock, Pennsylvania 16105
(724) 652-0511
www.HermesPress.com; info@hermespress.com

Cover image: Painting of The Phantom by George Wilson
Book design by Eileen Sabrina Herman
First printing, 2018

LCCN applied for 10 9 8 7 6 5 4 3 2 1 0
ISBN 978-161345-147-2
OCR and text editing by H + G Media and Eileen Sabrina Herman
Proof reading by Eileen Sabrina Herman

From Dan, Louise, Sabrina, Ruckus, and Noodle for D'zur and Mellow

Acknowledgements: This book would not be possible without the help, cooperation, patience, and kindness of many people. First and foremost in making this endeavor a reality are Ita Golzman and Frank Caruso at King Features. Thanks also to Pete Klaus and the late Ed Rhoades of "The Friends of the Phantom." Pete and Ed have provided us with resource material, contacts, information, and helpful insights into the strip and continue to be there when we have questions about the world of The Ghost Who Walks.

Editor's Note: There were several misspellings in the original text; those have been corrected with this reprint. However, the alternate spelling for the Singh pirates as Singg was kept to preserve the original format.

Printed in Canada

I wish to dedicate this book to those good friends and bold pioneers who first introduced The Phantom to Europe and Latin America so many years ago: Paul Winkler of Paris, the late Bjarne Steinsvik of Stockholm, Salvador Mendoza of Mexico City, and Percy Forster of Buenos Aires.

Lee Falk

The Story of THE PHANTOM and Killer's Town

CONTENTS

WITH THE PHANTOM, EVERYTHING IS POSSIBLE— EXCEPT BOREDOM

by
Francis Lacassin, Lecturer
The Sorbonne, Paris, France

When Lee Falk introduced into comic-strip format the imaginary and the fantastic with the figure of *Mandrake, The Magician*, it was apparent that he was contributing to what I describe to my students at the Sorbonne as "The Ninth Art." It was even more evident when he invented The Phantom, a figure who set the fashion for the masked and costumed Man of Justice,

On November 15, 1971, the oldest university in Europe, the Sorbonne, opened its doors to the comics. I was privileged to give, with the section of Graphic Arts, a weekly two-hour course in the History of the Aesthetics and Language of Comic Strips. Prior sessions had been devoted to the *Phantom*. The female students were drawn to the attractiveness and elegance of his figure; the men liked his masculinity and humor. To me, Lee Falk's stories— representing as they do the present-day *Thousand and One Nights*, fairy tales, *The Tales of the Knights of the Round Table*, etc.—adapt the epic poetry for the dreams and needs of an advanced and industrial civilization. For me the Phantom reincarnates Achilles, the valorous warrior of the Trojan War, and like a knight he wanders about the world in search of a crime to castigate or a wrong to right.

Lee Falk's art of storytelling is defined as much by the succinctness of the action, as by that of the dialogue. The text has not only a dry, terse quality, but also delicious humor. The humor shows itself in the action by the choice of daring ellipses: nothing remains but the strong points of the action. This allows the story to progress more rapidly and reduces the gestures of the hero to those which underlie his fantastic physical prowess. Falk gives the drama in a nutshell. A remarkable example is the resume done in four frames (in the comic strip) and placed at the beginning of each episode to recall the Phantom's origins. In four pictures, everything about the man is said, his romantic legend, his noble mission. Moreover, the new reader enters the fabulous world of Lee Falk, where nothing is real but everything is possible—except boredom.

Dressed in a soft hat and an overcoat with the collar upturned, the Phantom and his wolf, Devil, wander about the world, the cities of Europe, or, dressed in his eighteenth-century executioner's costume, he passes his time in the jungle. Wherever he is, he acts like a sorcerer of the fantastic. Under his touch, the real seems to crack and dreams Well through.

A masked ball in the Latin Quarter appears. In the Phantom's eyes it is the rendezvous of a redoubtable secret society of women. The jungle vegetation becomes the jewel box in which are hidden lost cities, sleeping gods, vampire queens, tournaments worthy of the Olympic Games. The geography, the flowers, the animals in their turn undergo a magical change brought on by the hero. A savage continent borders the edge of the Deep Woods. It is protected by a praetorian guard, the pygmies. The Skull Cave contains the treasures of war and the archives of his ancestors. All this occurs on a mythical continent which is not exactly Africa nor exactly Asia, because the tigers and lions are friends.

The genius of Lee Falk is to have known how to create a new *Odyssey*, with all of its fantastic color, but what is even more surprising is that it would be believable in the familiar settings of the modern world. The Phantom acts with the audacity of Ulysses and also with the nobility of a knight-errant. In contrast to Ulysses, and similarly to Sir Lancelot, he moves about in the world of his own free will among his peers. Lee Falk has not only managed to combine epic poetry with fairy tales and the stories of chivalry, he has made of the Phantom, in a jungle spared by colonialism, an agent of political equilibrium and friendship between races. In giving his hero an eternal mission, Lee Falk has made him so real, so near, so believable that he has made of him a man of all times. He will outlive him as Ulysses has outlived Homer. But in contrast to Ulysses, his adventures will continue after his creator is gone, because his creator has made of him an indispensable figure endowed with a life of his own. This is a privilege of which the heroes of written word cannot partake; no one has been able to imitate Homer.

However, the comic strip is the victim of a fragile medium, the newspaper. Because of this, some adventures of *The Phantom* have been lost and live only in the memory of their readers. This memory is difficult to communicate to others. Lee Falk has, therefore, given a new dimension to *The Phantom* by making of him the hero of a series of novels, introducing his origins and his first adventures to those who did not know him before.

This is not his least important accomplishment, but the most significant in my opinion is this: —in presenting to us The Phantom, as a friend, Lee Falk has taught us to dream, which is something no school in the world can teach.

Francis Lacassin
June, 1972 Paris

PROLOGUE

How It All Began

*O*ver four hundred years ago, a large British merchant ship was *attacked by Singg pirates off the remote shores of Bangalla. The captain of the trading vessel was a famous seafarer who, in his youth, had served as cabin boy to Christopher Columbus on his first voyage to discover the New World. With the captain was his son, Kit, a strong young man who idolized his father and hoped to follow him as a seafarer. But the pirate attack was disastrous. In a furious battle, the entire crew of the merchant ship was killed and the ship sank in flames. The sole survivor was young Kit who, as he fell off the burning ship, saw his father killed by a pirate. Kit was washed ashore, half-dead. Friendly pygmies found him and nursed him to health.*

One day, walking on the beach, he found a dead pirate dressed in his fathers clothes. He realized this was the pirate who had killed his father. Grief-stricken, he waited until vultures had stripped the body clean. Then on the skull of his father's murderer, he swore an oath by firelight as the pygmies watched. "I swear to devote my life to the destruction of piracy, greed, cruelty, and injustice – and my sons and their sons shall follow me."

This was the Oath of the Skull that Kit and his descendants would live by. In time, the pygmies led him to their home in the Deep Woods in the center of the jungle, where he found a large cave with many rocky chambers. The mouth of the cave, a natural formation formed by the water and wind of centuries, was curiously like a skull. This became his home, the Skull Cave. He soon adopted a mask and a strange costume. He found that the mystery and fear this inspired helped him in his endless battle against world-wide piracy. For he and his sons who followed became known as the nemesis of pirates everywhere, a mysterious man whose face no one ever saw, whose name no one knew, who worked alone.

As the years passed, he fought injustice wherever he found it. The first Phantom and the sons who followed found their wives in many places. One married a reigning queen, one a princess, one a beautiful red-haired barmaid. But whether queen or commoner, all followed their men back to the Deep Woods to live the strange but happy life of the wife of the Phantom. And of all the world, only she, wife of the Phantom and their children, could see his face.

Generation after generation was conceived and born, grew to manhood, and assumed the tasks of the father before him. Each wore the mask and costume. Folk of the jungle and the city and sea began to whisper that there was a man who could not die, a Phantom, a Ghost Who Walks. For they thought the Phantom was always the same man. A boy who saw the Phantom would see him again fifty years after; and he seemed the same. And he would tell his son and his grandson; and then his son and grandson would see the Phantom fifty years after that. And he would seem the same. So the legend grew. The Man Who Cannot Die. The Ghost Who Walks. The Phantom.

The Phantom did not discourage this belief in his immortality. Always working alone against tremendous – sometimes almost impossible – odds, he found that the awe and fear the legend inspired was a great help in his endless battle against evil. Only his friends, the pygmies, knew the truth. To compensate for their tiny stature, the pygmies, mixed deadly poisons for use on their weapons in hunting or defending themselves. It was rare that they were forced to defend themselves. Their deadly poisons were known through the jungle, and they and their home, the Deep Woods, were dreaded and avoided. Another reason to stay away from the Deep Woods – it soon became known that this was a home of the Phantom, and none wished to trespass.

Through the ages, the Phantoms created several more homes, or hideouts, in various parts of the world. Near the Deep Woods was the Isle of Eden, where the Phantom taught all animals to live in peace. In the southwest desert of the New World, the Phantoms created an eyrie on a high, steep mesa that was thought by the Indians to be haunted by evil spirits and became known as "Walker's Table" – for the Ghost Who Walks. In Europe, deep in the crumbling cellars of ancient castle ruins, the Phantom had another hideout from which to strike against evildoers.

But the Skull Cave in the quiet of the Deep Woods remained the true home of the Phantom. Here, in a rocky chamber, he kept his chronicles, written records of all his adventures. Phantom after Phantom faithfully recorded their experiences in the large folio volumes. Another chamber contained the costumes of all the generations of Phantoms. Other chambers contained the vast treasures of the Phantom acquired over the centuries, used only in the endless battle against evil.

Thus twenty generations of Phantoms lived, fought, and died – usually violently – as they fulfilled their oath. Jungle folk, sea folk and city folk believed him the same man, the Man Who Cannot Die. Only the pygmies knew that always, a day would come when their great friend would die. Then, alone, a strong young son would carry his father to the burial crypt of his ancestors where all Phantoms rested. As the pygmies waited outside, the young man would emerge from the cave, wearing the mask, the costume, and the skull ring of the Phantom; his carefree, happy days as the Phantom's son were over. And the pygmies would chant their age-old chant, "The Phantom is dead. Long live the Phantom."

The story of Killer's Town is an adventure of the Phantom of our time—the twenty-first generation of his line. He has inherited the traditions and responsibilities created by four centuries of Phantom ancestors. One ancestor created the Jungle Patrol. Thus, today, our Phantom is the mysterious and unknown commander of this elite corps. In the jungle, he is known and loved as The Keeper of the Peace. On his right hand is the Skull Ring that leaves his mark— the Sign of the Skull—known and feared by evildoers everywhere. On his left hand—closer to the heart—is his "good mark" ring. Once given, the mark grants the lucky bearer protection by the Phantom, and it is equally known and respected. And to good people and criminals alike in the jungle, on the seven seas, and in the cities of the world he is the Phantom, the Ghost Who Walks, the Man Who Cannot Die.

Lee Falk
New York 1973

CHAPTER 1

With the precision that comes from long practice, the Governor-General of New Metropolis launched a squirt of tobacco juice that traveled the full length of his long skinny body to hit a wasp hovering near his bare, dirty big toe. The blast hit the insect broadside, dropping it onto a heap of trash and garbage just over the edge of the veranda. The Governor-General chuckled triumphantly, took a gulp of warm beer from a can, and with his free hand scratched several exposed parts of his body to relieve a chronic itch.

It was not only his big toe that was dirty. It is unlikely that there was a bar of soap in any of the forty-seven empty rooms of the mansion. The Governor-General, stretched out on a sagging chaise longue, wore only ragged trousers and a tom shirt that were dirty as the skin beneath. His hair and beard were matted and scraggly. But as he reclined on the creaky chaise longue, all the land, that stretched before his bleary eyes was his.

Beyond the trash and weeds that covered what had been the front lawn of the Governor-General's mansion was a street with three blocks of stone and wood buildings. All the glass in the windows had long since been shattered. Broken doors and shutters banged and sagged on rusty hinges. Roofs and walls had collapsed. Grass and bushes grew on the street and sidewalk, uprooting the concrete slabs. There were butterflies in the grass, lizards in the weeds, spiders on webs in windows and doors, a hungry cat searching in the rubble, a bird pausing on the roof. Beyond that, no life stirred.

New Metropolis had been a ghost town for twenty-five years. Gold had been discovered nearby, creating the short-lived boom town. During its brief period of glory. New Metropolis burst with life—miners, their women, and all the rest who came to find their fortunes. But the gold vein was shallow, quickly exhausted, and despite a frantic search there was no more gold. So the town died.

While it died, one man gradually acquired all the property for less and less, buying some, winning some at cards, stealing the rest He finally owned the entire town, having some dim notion that the boom years might return. They never did.

A ghost town is not unusual. They are found all over the world, usually with histories similar to this one. But New Metropolis was unique in one way. The area, perhaps a thousand acres overall, was not under the sovereignty of any nation. It was a no-man's land—on the border of Bangalla and the neighboring Lower Gamma. Both nations had disputed the property and at one time sent troops who glared at each other from a safe distance, then withdrew, both deciding it was not worth fighting over.

The owner of New Metropolis, elected mayor and self-appointed Governor-General, Matthew Crumb, had watched the soldiers from the second-floor ballroom window of his forty-seven-room mansion. The mansion was in better shape in those days. A few of the rooms were still furnished, and one of the fifteen bathrooms still worked. He watched with some anxiety. He knew the politicians of both countries, and he also knew that, whichever country won, he would lose. It was with vast relief that he saw them withdraw, though he was furious when he learned the reason— neither country thought his town was worth firing one bullet to get.

The twenty-five years passed. The boom never returned. Matthew Crumb and New Metropolis sank together in apathy into the jungle. Time, moths, termites, rust, and alcohol did their slow destruction.

Governor-General Matthew Crumb blinked and stared, and listened alertly. Was it possible? There were remains of an old wall and a gaping gateway at the end of the street An automobile was entering his domain. Butterflies, lizards, spiders, birds, and the cat scurried into hiding. This was an amazing event. No strangers had come here in years.

Two men got out of the car. They were well dressed in dark clothes and hats—city men—and from the sound of them not of Bangalla. They looked at the faded glories of New Metropolis.

"This is the place," said one of them.

"Phooey," said the other. "Are you sure?"

"Sure."

The two men walked to the broken fence of the mansion and slowly approached the veranda, avoiding the trash, garbage, and animal offal. Matthew Crumb, remaining on his broken chaise longue, watched them as they came near. He sipped the beer slowly, barely interested. Whatever they wanted, directions probably, they would ask. They didn't matter to him, one way or another. The men stopped at the edge of the porch. One of them had soiled his highly polished brown shoes, and muttered an obscenity.

"Are you Matthew Crumb?" he said.

"I am."

"We want to talk to you."

The Governor-General of New Metropolis lowered his beer can and wiped his mouth with a filthy sleeve.

"Go ahead and talk," he said.

CHAPTER 2

The headline tells the story:

Killer Koy Loses Appeal
Ganglord and top aides to be Deported

Killer Koy was proud of his nickname. He had earned it. During his violent career up to that point, it was alleged that he had committed four murders himself and ordered a dozen more. He was indicted four times but was never found guilty. The cases were dismissed for lack of evidence —witnesses against him forgot, or disappeared. In those years, Koy was involved in almost every major crime known to man. Robbery, arson, extortion, bribery, assault, drugs, prostitution, and, of course, murder. He was finally nailed down and sentenced to ten years in a federal penitentiary for income-tax evasion, just like his idol, the late Al Capone. He served the sentence with three years off for good behavior. He came out, arrogant and roaring mad, determined never to spend another hour in jail.

But he was promptly hauled before the Immigration Service to face deportation. It seems that Koy, an immigrant, had never taken the time to become a citizen. He hired a battery of lawyers and fought the deportation from court to court, but finally lost—to the relief of practically everybody in the fifty states of the Union. This created a new problem. Nobody wanted him. His native

Rumania took one horrified look at his record and said no. Thirty other nations on both sides of the Atlantic also said no. Koy was livid.

"Find me a place," he roared at his hard working-aides —a polite name for thugs.

"We're trying," said one aide. "So far, thirty places said no."

"There are a lot more countries," said another aide hopefully. "We'll find one."

"Not a big one, a little one," said Koy. "A place where I can operate—without law."

"No law? Like where—the North Pole?"

"No North Pole. A warm place," shouted Koy. The aides left him in his cell; he was now being detained by the Immigration Service.

"Make it fast I've had enough of bars," he called after them.

When Koy said fast, he meant fast. His thugs worked frantically. They contacted every criminal gang in the western world. They tried South America, Asia, and Africa. They tried Bangalla. They found New Metropolis.

Eagle and Sport were the two Koy aides who found the place. Eagle was a disbarred lawyer; Sport was a former professional wrestler and dance-hall bouncer. Brains and brawn.

"You own this place?" said Eagle.

"Lock, stock, and barrel," said Matthew Crumb, adding a belch for emphasis.

"Want to sell it?"

"What part?"

"All of it."

Matthew chuckled and had another gulp.

"This rubbish heap? You're either crazy or pulling my leg."

Sport growled, "Want me to work him over?"

"No, stupid. We're serious. We want the whole place. How much?"

"Hell, I'd settle for a case of booze," said the Governor-General.

"You got a deal," said Eagle.

Matthew's eyes opened wide for the first time. He sat up.

"Wait a minute. I got a thousand acres. I want a good price."

"Don't worry. You got a good deal," said Eagle.

"Bangalla? Where in hell's that?" asked Koy.

They showed it to him on the map, which meant nothing to

him.

"It's in the jungle," explained Eagle.

"How about the law."

"No law."

"How come no law?"

"The whole place is yours. You're the law."

"Me?" said Koy, excited for the first time. "You sure, Eagle?"

"Sure," said Eagle, holding up his briefcase. "I've got the papers."

"What do they call this place?" said Koy.

"New Metropolis."

"That's a lousy name."

"It's your place. You can give it a new name."

"Yeah, I've got to get a good new name for my town," said Killer Koy, grinning.

CHAPTER 3

The departure of Killer Koy and his entourage did not go unnoticed. Reporters and TV cameras were at the airport, as well as immigration officials to make sure Koy actually left.

"Where you going, Killer?" a TV reporter asked, shoving a microphone at Koy.

"None of your damned business," said Koy, snarling a few choice epithets into the live microphone, which shocked a mid-afternoon housewives' audience from coast to coast.

Koy's arrival at the Bangalla airport also did not go unnoticed. Black Police Chief Togando watched the six toughs who came down the plane's stairs with Koy. All carried heavy-looking hand luggage. They left the airport with two dozen trunks and boxes. Four taxis carried them through the town and into its outskirts. Chief Togando followed in a squad car as far as the jungle's edge and watched with surprise as the cars turned into the jungle, onto a dirt road known as the Phantom Trail. What would these men do in the jungle, he wondered. Perhaps they carried camping equipment, though they didn't look like campers. He left a man to see if they returned. The jungle was not in his jurisdiction.

"That's the place," said Eagle proudly.

Koy stared at the ghost town. It was already being transformed as a small army of workmen moved among the ruined buildings.

"That's my town?" said Koy in disbelief. "That dump heap?" He turned angrily on Eagle. "Is this your great idea?"

"Patience, Killer," said Eagle, retreating a step. "They're fixing it up. Wait till they finish it."

"Yeah, meantime, am I supposed to sleep under a bush?" shouted Koy.

"Now take it easy, boss," said Sport in his deep rumbling voice. "Eagle got you a fancy suite at the hotel in town."

"Yeah. We stay there till this is ready. You'll love it."

A barefoot man tottered toward them. He tottered because he was drunk.

"Mr. Eagle," he called. "Where's my money?"

"Who's that bum?" growled Koy.

"Matthew Crumb, the guy we bought this place from," said Eagle.

"Mr. Crumb, this is Mr. Koy, the new owner," said Eagle.

Koy looked contemptuously at Crumb, the ragged pants and soiled shirt, dirt from head to foot, tobacco juice leaking from his mouth.

"Pleased to meet you," said Crumb, putting out his hand.

Koy chewed his cigar, looked stonily at Crumb, then spit out a wad of tobacco that hit Crumb's waist. Crumb pulled back his hand, and retreated a step from the menacing face of the new owner.

"My money?" he said.

"You'll get all that's coming to you," said Eagle.

"My room, too. Don't forget my room," said Crumb anxiously.

"What room?" demanded Koy.

"Part of the deal," said Eagle apologetically. "He wanted a place to live. I promised him he could have a room in the new hotel."

Koy looked at the anxious watery eyes, at the trembling tobacco-stained mouth of the barefoot derelict. Koy knew bums. He'd known them all his life.

"Sure," he said, suddenly gentle. "Why not?"

Then he looked around at the alien jungle, the big trees, the strange colors. "Let's get back to town," he said.

Mawitaan's principle hotel, the Queen's Plaza—the name was a relic of the old colonial days—was in the center of town. It was a large sprawling comfortable place with huge rooms, high ceilings with revolving fans, broad colorful gardens. Koy felt more at home. Modern plumbing, wall-to-wall carpeting, room service. Liquor and ice were served, the men took off their coats and shoes, and were about to order lunch when Police Chief Togando knocked politely and entered. The Chief was black and his accent was strange, but he was a cop. Koy and his men were silent and wary.

"What are you doing here, Mr. Koy?" said the Chief.

"Passing through," said Koy.

"You all have visitor's visas. They expire in three months."

"We know that, Chief," said Eagle brightly.

"We're private citizens, and we like privacy," said Koy, glaring at the Chief.

The jungle-bred Togando was not to be put down by a foreign hoodlum.

"No funny business in this town, Mr. Koy. We obey the law here. We don't want any trouble from you," said the Chief quietly, his fingers idly playing with his gunbelt.

Koy nodded. The chief looked coolly at the standing men —Eagle, Sport, the tall one called Slim, the fat one called Fats, the bald man called Baldy, the stocky one with curly hair called Spaghetti—a walking rogues gallery.

"Good afternoon," said the Chief politely, and left. Koy spat on the carpet, smashed his burning cigar into the veneer finish of an end table, and swore.

"That damned cop," he growled. "I'd like to let him have it."

"Easy, Killer," said Eagle. "We're in his country."

"Not for long," said Killer. "Where's my lunch?"

Chief Togando's department policed the capital city of Mawitaan and its suburbs. Beyond that lay a thousand miles of jungle, bordered by seven nations. This was policed by the Jungle Patrol, an elite organization, two and a half centuries old, that was financially supported by all seven nations. This area of the world had been a haven for centuries for pirates, bandits, and escaped criminals. The Patrol's jurisdiction covered the long jungle borders and extended ten miles deep. A vast territory. The deep jungle, the land of the interior tribes, was beyond Patrol jurisdiction. It was ruled by the tribal chiefs and, it was whispered, by another whose name and person were lost in mystery. But more of him later.

Chief Togando was troubled by the memory of the men he saw in the hotel suite. He was used to dealing with criminals, but these weren't like the usual run. He had sensed vicious brutality backed by money and a widespread powerful organization. He took his worries to his counterpart in the Patrol, Colonel Randolph Weeks, commanding officer (but not Commander) of the Jungle Patrol. Weeks was a cool, unflappable leader who had spent most of his adult life in this international patrol and had risen from the ranks to become its colonel.

"What's a big-time hood like Koy doing in our little town, I keep asking myself," said Chief Togando, as he sat in Weeks's office at Jungle Patrol headquarters. "But I get no answers."

He described his meeting with Koy and the gang. "A frightening crowd." Weeks nodded.

"Here on a visitor's visa, all of them," said Weeks. "The question is, where do they go from here? We know practically every country on earth has refused them a visa. The Bangalla foreign office was generous enough—or foolish enough—to give them a temporary visa. Maybe that was a mistake."

"Yes, what worries me is why did they pick this place? They went directly from the airport into the jungle along the Phantom Trail. Why, or how far in, I don't know," said Togando.

"Neither of us has any answers," said Weeks. "I'll get Koy over here. Maybe he can supply some." He talked into his phone.

"Send Sergeant Hill in, please," he said.

A husky young patrolman entered, walked smartly to the desk, and stood at attention. There is no saluting in the Patrol.

"Sergeant, a man named Koy is at the Queen's Plaza. Will you bring him to my office? I want to see him," said Weeks.

"Yes sir," said Sergeant Dave Hill.

"He is the gangster."

"Yes sir, I know."

"Some of his men are with him. Perhaps you need help."

"How many men, sir?" said Sergeant Hill.

Weeks glanced inquiringly at Chief Togando.

"Koy and six others," said the Chief.

"I'll manage it, sir," said Sergeant Dave Hill, smiling.

There was an old adage in the patrol: *One patrolman can handle ten criminals.* True or not, they believed it. It was a fact that the patrolmen were the most carefully selected elite corps on earth. A thousand young men applied for entrance each year from all over the world. After rigorous physical and mental tests, only the top ten were accepted.

"Right away, Sergeant Hill," said Colonel Weeks.

"Yes sir."

Killer Koy was still grumbling about Chief Togando when Sergeant Dave Hill knocked politely, then entered. Koy was having his lunch. Eagle spoke to Dave Hill at the door, then asked him to wait in the anteroom and reported to Koy. Though the doors were closed, Dave could hear Koy's angry roar. Eagle returned, white-faced.

"He says we've already seen the police chief," said Eagle.

"We're not police. We're Jungle Patrol. Our Colonel Weeks wants to see Mr. Koy."

"Sorry, not today. Mr. Koy is busy," said Eagle, blocking the inner door.

Dave Hill brushed him aside. Koy was seated at the table, a chicken leg in his hand. Three other men seated on a sofa got up as Dave entered. Koy stared at him, speechless for the moment.

"Sorry to break in, but I have my orders. I'm Sergeant Hill of the Jungle Patrol. Our Colonel Weeks wants to see you, Mr. Koy."

Koy glared at Dave Hill. Patrolmen wear khaki shorts, high socks and short boots, tan shirts, pith helmets. No guns, except during jungle duty. Dave Hill was unarmed.

Koy glared and swore, a string of obscenities that ended with ". . . and I've got no time for tin colonels and Boy Scouts. Get lost before we throw you out!"

Dave Hill moved forward swiftly. He kicked the table over, spilling dishes, glasses, and plates all over Koy and the floor. The violence of the move threw Koy back in his chair so that he fell against the wall. Before the other men could move, Dave Hill had grabbed Koy by his collar and produced handcuffs from a back pocket.

"On your feet, you miserable hood," barked Sergeant Hill. "Are you coming with me, or do I have to put on these bracelets?" The other men had started forward. The sight of the gleaming handcuffs made them pause. All had served time in jail and the handcuffs meant the law, authority. Then Eagle held up a restraining hand.

"Of course we'll go along with you, Sergeant," he said. "We want no trouble here, do we, Mr. Koy?"

Koy breathed deeply.

"Right. We'll go along with you. Boy Scout."

"Good thinking," said Sergeant Dave Hill.

Koy stood before Colonel Weeks, lighting a cigar. He threw the burning match on Weeks's polished desk. Weeks put it out, and tossed it into an ashtray. Eagle, at the side of the room, watched Koy nervously.

"We already saw the police chief. He runs this town. Why do I have to see you?" said Koy.

"This is not the police department. This is the Jungle Patrol. We cover the jungle borders. You and your men were seen entering the jungle on the Phantom trail. That makes you our business."

Koy glanced at Eagle.

"We took a ride. Do we need your permission?" said Eagle.

"Not ordinarily," said Colonel Weeks. "In the case of known criminals, we ask questions."

"You can't talk to me like that. I did my time. I'm a free man," shouted Koy.

Colonel Weeks looked at him quietly.

"No need to shout, Mr. Koy. My hearing is quite adequate for normal conversation."

Koy held back his anger. The quiet manner and aristocratic British accent of this smooth, gray-haired soldier infuriated him.

"What is your business in the jungle? Why did you drive directly there upon your arrival at the airport?"

Koy looked at Eagle, his mouthpiece.

"We'd been in the air a long time. We wanted a ride. We wanted to see the jungle. That's all," said Eagle.

"Yeah, that's it," said Koy.

The Colonel studied the two men for a moment.

"That's it, for now," he said softly. "Remember, this is our country. There's no room for your mob here."

"Who needs a jungle?" snorted Koy. "I'm a city boy."

"Your visa expires in three months. There will be no extension. Not an hour. Good day," said Colonel Weeks. Koy left the office muttering. Back in the hotel suite, he exploded.

"That idiot! If I ever get my hands on him!" he roared.

"Easy, Killer," said Eagle. "He's the law."

Koy turned on him.

"The law?" he shouted. "I said I wanted a place with no law. Jungle patrol, police chief—here they've got two laws."

He swung his heavy fist, hitting Eagle in the face. The slim lawyer fell back onto the couch, then onto the floor. Koy was boiling with anger. He pulled a switch-blade knife from his pocket and snapped open the long blade. His eyes were wild as he glared at the fallen Eagle.

"Two laws—that policeman—that idiot Colonel!" he shouted.

Eagle stared at him, paralyzed with fear. He'd seen this murderous rage in this boss before.

"Jeez, Killer, take it easy," he managed to choke out. "You're getting your own town. You'll be the law, the only law."

"Yeah," rumbled big Sport, coming forward to protect Eagle, "your own town. Killer. Call it Killer's Town."

"Yes, Killer's Town," said Eagle quickly, and the other watching men picked it up, making laughing sounds, but their eyes remained hard, watching Killer's big knife.

"Yeah, Killer's Town," said Koy. "That's good. Killer's Town."

He breathed deeply, and walked to the window, closing the knife as he tried to recover from his maniacal rage.

Eagle got slowly to his feet with Sport's help, and felt his throat. That had been a close one.

In Jungle Patrol Headquarters, Colonel Weeks and Sergeant Hill discussed their visitors.

"Murderous hoods, all armed. How do you figure them, sir?" asked Sergeant Dave Hill.

"Don't know yet, Dave," Weeks replied. It was rarely that he called a patrolman by his first name. "I was wrong to send you alone into that snake pit."

"I managed, sir," said Dave Hill. "For a minute there, it didn't look good."

"That Koy deserves his nickname. He's a bad one. We'll keep an eye on them."

"Yes sir."

CHAPTER 4

The work at New Metropolis went on at a furious rate around the clock. Construction, remodeling, demolition. Big fires burned night and day, consuming the almost endless trash, rotten timbers, and junk. Trucks rumbled in at all hours loaded with materials. Some deliveries were made by boat. A finger of salt water from Bangalla Bay reached in to touch the property. There were old crumbling wharfs and a deep-water anchorage where the ore-carrying boats had been loaded in the old days. Workmen were housed in a small city of tents. There were no union rules to delay matters here. They worked night and day with time out for meals and sleep. The work was supervised by two of Roy's specialists, Slim and Spaghetti, both of whom he had met in prison.

Slim, an architect, had served time for embezzlement Spaghetti, a former construction foreman, had been sentenced after he tried to settle a labor dispute with a sledge hammer. The union delegate, on the receiving end of the sledge hammer, spent six months in a hospital; Spaghetti got six years in jail. Sport, the ex-bouncer, moved among the workmen with a club, discouraging any cigarette or coffee breaks. Koy was not seen during this time, remaining in seclusion in his hotel suite, entertained with endless sessions of poker, which he always won, and occasional visits from "ladies" of the town.

Matthew Crumb watched all this activity in dazed amazement. He had rescued his sagging chaise longue from a pile of trash just as workmen were about to burn it. He dragged it into a clear space among the weeds and settled himself there with a case of beer. The never-ending cases of beer, appearing at his side as if by a miracle, were supplied by the indulgent Eagle. In answer to Crumb's repeated question of "where's my money?" Eagle would nod and wink and send over another case of beer. From this happy vantage point, Crumb watched the turmoil that was transforming the ghost town.

All this activity could not be kept secret, nor was there any attempt to do so. Word reached town of the construction work going on in the jungle. There was speculation that the attempt was being made to reopen the old gold mines. Others said that timber interests were at work. But since the area was far beyond the city of Mawitaan and its suburbs, none of the official bureaus was involved.

A casual watch had been kept on Koy at the hotel, both by the police and the Jungle Patrol. Some of his henchmen were no longer observed there. It was assumed they had left the country. But it was obvious that Koy himself remained in seclusion in the hotel. As long as he behaved himself, there was no reason to interfere with him. Besides, his time in Bangalla would soon be up.

The morning before that final day, Colonel Weeks, Chief Togando, and the Immigration Department discussed the matter by phone. It was agreed they would jointly escort Koy to the airport and make sure he took off. All were relieved that the ganglord's stay in Mawitaan had caused no trouble. But the next day, when a patrolman inquired at the front desk for Koy, the clerk told him Koy and his party had checked out during the night, leaving no forwarding address. They'd left in three big limousines, with all their luggage and a few "ladies" of the town who had joined the group.

Koy had not disappeared. The Patrol quickly learned where he had gone. To that old ghost town, New Metropolis.

"What's he trying to prove?" said Colonel Weeks on the telephone to Chief Togando. "That place is still Bangalla." He was wrong about that, as he was to learn. He called in Sergeant Dave Hill.

"Our man skipped into the woods, to that old town," said the Colonel. "Who is that old man out there?"

"Matthew Crumb, sir. I just looked it up. He calls himself the Governor-General," he added, grinning.

"Go out there and escort Koy and his crowd back to the airport. Take eight men, with automatic weapons. If Koy resists, use whatever force is necessary."

"Yes sir."

The three Patrol vehicles sped along the bumpy jungle road known as the Phantom trail. (Nobody in town seemed to know where that name had come from. Anybody in the jungle could have told them.) The road seemed bumpier than ever. As the Patrol cars reached the last turn, they stopped to examine a large new sign at the side of the road.

KILLER'S TOWN
Private—No Admittance

That was good for a laugh among the patrolmen, and they rode on. What they saw next was no laughing matter. They were amazed.

A new little town was growing behind high new walls, topped with spikes and broken glass. A gate of heavy iron bars was closed and locked. A man armed with an automatic rifle peered at them from the gate. Behind him, on the newly paved street, there was much activity. Towering over the smaller new buildings was the remodeled forty-seven- room mansion, now bearing a large neon sign—The Killer Hilton.

Sergeant Hill went to the gate, gun in hand.

"Jungle Patrol," he said. "Open up."

The guard, hulking Sport, glared at him.

"You saw the sign back there. No admittance. This is private property."

"None of your lip. Unlock this gate or we'll blow it open. We want Koy."

A voice called to him from the background. Through the bars, he saw Koy standing on a second-floor balcony near the hotel sign.

"You heard him, Boy Scout. Ever hear of trespassing? This is my town. You got no right here. Blow!" shouted Koy. The ganglord wasn't angry now. He appeared delighted with himself, and the men with him laughed appreciatively. Hill hesitated. Koy's words seemed to carry the ring of truth. A raggedy man shuffled toward the gates. He was drinking from a beer can as he walked.

"That's right. All his now," said Matthew Crumb.

"The Governor-General," said Hill. "What is all this. Crumb?"

"I sold it to him. The whole place," said Matthew.

"So what?" said Hill. "You're under arrest Koy. You and your whole gang," he shouted.

Koy and the men on the balcony laughed.

"You can't arrest me, Boy Scout. Your law's no good here. I'm the law here now. Tell that to your scoutmaster. Colonel Weeks—the idiot!" More laughter from the balcony.

Hill went back to the other patrolmen.

"What do you think? Shall we break in?" he said.

"There is something about this place that's special, I seem to remember," said an older patrolman. "An independent enclave, something like that. Bangalla almost fought a war over it ten years ago."

"We'll go back and check it out," said Hill. He turned back to the gate and shouted to Koy, still visible on the balcony.

"We'll be back, Koy."

They could still hear the thugs' shouts and laughter as they made the turn at the new sign:

KILLER'S TOWN
Private—No Admittance

They checked the records. It was true. The Jungle Patrol had no authority over New Metropolis, now Killer's Town. Neither had the Mawitaan police. Nor the Bangallan military. Nobody had. It was an independent free port.

"How in hell did that happen?" bellowed Colonel Weeks. It was rare that Weeks, a quiet and religious man, either roared or used profanity.

"He pulled one on us," said Chief Togando bitterly.

"He checked that place out before he bought it. Must have spent a fortune on it," said Sergeant Hill.

"He's safe inside, said Togando. "But if he comes out . . ."

"Right, he's harmless in there. Might as well be in jail," said Colonel Weeks, suddenly cheerful.

"Right!" said Sergeant Hill. He's made his own jail."

They were happy about that for a few minutes, then Colonel Weeks became somber.

"Why would he go to all that trouble? Just to make a hideout for himself? One house would be enough. Why a whole little town? What's Koy really up to?"

They would all find out soon.

CHAPTER 5

The word spread fast in the right places. Roy's men saw to that. The word was—a luxury hideout, safe from cops, narcs, Feds, Scotland Yard, Surety, Interpol, MP, SP, Jungle Patrol— in short, safe from the law of all nations.

Across Bangalla's southern border, in the prosperous little capital of Lower Gamma, the National Bank was robbed in a daring daylight robbery with dynamite and automatic rifles. Two guards and one bystander killed, four wounded. A half million in gold bullion had arrived at the bank from the refinery the day before, intended for the metal artisans of India. The four robbers, plus two drivers, escaped into high-powered cars across the Bangalla border. The crossing occurred at noon when, as everyone knew, the sentries were always away from their posts having lunch. The Lower Gamma police pursued, well behind, as far as the border. When the Jungle Patrol was alerted by radio some time later, the trail was cold. The thieves had vanished into the jungle.

They had "vanished" behind the high iron gates of Killer's Town. Roy was waiting for them as they rolled up to the shining new Killer Hilton. The thieves, a mixture of Frenchmen and Dutchmen, were excited by their successful adventure, shouting happily, roaring with laughter at the humorous incidents of the robbery, like the fat man who caught a dum-dum in the belly. "You shoulda seen his face."

"You boys had a big caper," said Roy as soon as they had quieted down at the bar and were gulping whiskey.

The men agreed noisily and began to tell him about it He listened for a moment.

"Radio says you got a half million in gold," he went on. They nodded, looking through the window at the trunks of their cars parked outside.

"You want to hide out here?" Roy asked.

They grinned at him. That had been the idea, even before they started, arranged by mutual friends.

"We'll take you in . . .for half the loot," said Roy.

They stared at him. Half!

The gang looked quickly for their guns. Roy's men had taken them from the cars, and were standing with them behind him.

"Half? Jeez, Killer," said the gang's spokesman, a Parisian called Frenchy.

Koy shrugged and waved to the jungle outside.

"Rather go out there and find another place?"

The gang put their heads together.

"What do you think, Dutch?" said Frenchy to another thug. (The underworld is not bright about names. A fat man is Fats; a skinny man is Slim; a man with scars on his face is Scarface; a man whose name sounds like banana is Banana.)

What else could they do? They agreed.

"Show the boys to their rooms—with baths," said Killer Koy grandly. His share of the half million went into the safe. The remainder soon found its way to Killer's gambling casino next door. Money that went into the casino rarely came out. . .

A short time later, there was excitement at Killer's wharf. As Koy and his men watched, a large amphibian plane landed with a splash. They cheered and passed champagne around as the pilot climbed out on the dock. He was a dashing fellow with a small mustache and wavy hair, a favorite with airline stewardessess until he had been fired from the airline and the Pilots' Association for being drunk on the job. He had a name but he would be known to Koy and his thugs only as "Pilot." Anything more was too much trouble to remember.

"How about that. A cool million!" shouted Killer.

"Wow!" said everybody.

"Three million new," said Eagle. "We got a good deal."

"It can fly across the ocean," said Spaghetti.

"From New York or London or Paris?" asked Moogar, the only local black thug in this gang of foreign whites.

"From anywhere. And it's ours!" said Sport loudly.

Killer Koy looked at him coldly.

"Mine," he said.

The plane and pilot were kept busy in the following months. Clients came from London, Rome, Johannesburg; one came all the way from Hong Kong, a smiling Oriental with two suitcases full of opium. On Manhattan's West Side, in the famous jewel mart, there was a million-dollar diamond heist. The robbery had been carefully planned by Fingers, a veteran safecracker, fresh from a ten-year stretch at Sing Sing. It was his boast that he could open any combination safe in the world.

The heist was carefully planned because Fingers had no desire to return to Sing Sing, and had prearranged a trip to Killer's Town with his loot. Fingers cased the job meticulously. The night watchman had a coffee break for ten minutes every night at exactly one o'clock. That was more time than Fingers needed to open a padlock on an alley door, get to the diamond vault, open it, and get out So he figured. He actually did it in seven minutes. As insurance, he took along a young up-and-coming thug named Pretty as lookout.

Pretty was a strong young man with curly blond hair, blue eyes, and the face of a Botticelli angel. He was also as dangerous, unpredictable, and deadly as a rattlesnake. His beautiful face had kept him in trouble since he was twelve, with girls who wouldn't let him alone, and with boys who provoked him to fight His childhood home in a Brooklyn ghetto had been sordid. He had never known his father, and it is doubtful if his mother was certain who, among her acquaintances, had had the dubious honor of fathering him. She was an alcoholic who brought men home. As a small boy, Pretty watched these drunken scenes while cowering in his cot pretending to sleep. At twelve, he had a fight with one of the men, a sailor who tried to beat him. Pretty stabbed him with a kitchen knife and ran away. From that time on, he lived in the streets, avoiding school and the law as best he could. He was finally arrested for assault and rape, and sent to reform school. After two days there, the authorities sent him to a mental hospital, where he was diagnosed as a psychopathic personality prone to violence. Pretty escaped from the place one night, and promised himself never to be caught again. He progressed from petty thievery to street mugging to holdups. It was soon learned that behind that angelic face was the cold and twisted mind of a relentless killer. The old night watchman in the jewelry mart learned about Pretty that night. He returned from his coffee break in eight minutes instead of the usual ten. He met them in the alley as Fingers was closing the padlock. The old man was unarmed. It was a simple matter to tie and gag him, which Fingers was about to do. But Pretty shot the old man dead. Fingers took one horrified look at the cold angelic face then, clutching his suitcase, fled from the alley to the waiting car. Pretty followed. As luck would have it, a police squad car was passing and the lone cop at the wheel had heard the shot. He jumped out, gun in hand, as Fingers and Pretty reached the curb. Pretty shot him dead, too. A pretty girl in hot pants, heading back to her hotel room after a stint in the streets, saw the shooting and screamed. As he stepped into the car, Pretty fired at her. The shot knocked her to the sidewalk as the car sped away.

"You lunatic! What did you do that for?" shouted Fingers.

Pretty's eyes were shining and he was smiling and breathing hard, like a man who's just won a tough set of tennis.

"No witnesses," he said hoarsely.

These were his first killings. Later on, he would be less excited. The car sped on to the remote dock where the big white amphibian plane was waiting in the bay. The plan had been for Pretty to drive the car back to town after Fingers's departure. Pilot was waiting at the dock with one of the blond "ladies" from Killer's Town who'd become his special friend.

"Everything okay?" he said, looking at the suitcase.

"Yeah. Let's get out fast," said Fingers. "The whole town will be looking for you," he said to Pretty.

"And for you," said Pretty, grinning, as Fingers swore. I'll go with you, wherever that is."

"I'm only supposed to have one passenger," said Pilot

"Now you got two," said Pretty.

"Killer said one," said Pilot stubbornly.

Pretty put a gun under Pilot's chin, and stared into his eyes. Pretty had pale-blue eyes, like a wolf.

"Two," he said.

"Okay," said Pilot with a weak laugh. "I see what you mean."

When the plane reached the wharf at Killer's Town, after a stop in the Azores, Koy was waiting. He looked appreciatively at Fingers's suitcase. The radio had already brought him news of the successful heist, and also of the murders.

"Who did the bang-bang?" said Koy.

Fingers gestured to Pretty who was breathing the tropical air and staring at the palm trees. This was his first time away from concrete and asphalt.

"This is Pretty," said Fingers.

The two looked at each other. Young killer—old killer.

"You want a room here?" said Koy.

"Sure," said Pretty.

"It'll cost you two hundred a day."

"Okay. See my banker," said Pretty, and strolled off following Pilot and the girl.

"What's with that kid, Fingers?"

"His first time out, he knocked off the old man and a cop. I don't know if the girl died. He didn't have to shoot the old man. Then nothing would have happened."

"Why did he do it? Buck fever?"

"No, Killer. I think he liked it," said Fingers.

Koy looked thoughtfully at the retreating figures, then nodded. "A mad dog. I know that kind. I can use him, but he'll need watching."

Not all refugees who came to Killer's Town had money. There was a jailbreak at Bangalla's penitentiary. Two lifers escaped from Death Row. They surprised a guard, disarmed him, then shot him, and got away over the wall. There was a Lovers' Lane a short distance away, a little road in a wooded area favored by romantic couples. The escaped cons found such a couple in an open car in eaeh other's arms. Alarm sirens and barking dogs could be heard in the distance as the search for the escaped men began. This probably saved the girl from an attack. The frightened couple were left on the road as their car raced off. Guards found them a short time later and pursued the stolen car into the jungle. The trail led to the new-walled town, Killer's Town.

The police cars screeched to a stop at the closed gate, their sirens wailing, flashing green-red searchlights revolving, as they roared through amplified megaphones.

"Open up. We want those two men."

Laughter answered them, then a voice also using a power megaphone—Koy's voice.

"Get lost, fuzz." More laughter. Female and male.

"Those two are lifers, escaped murderers," shouted the chief guard.

"Don't tell us your problems. This is private property. No trespassing. Get lost, fuzz."

More raucous laughter, male and female. The guards debated the possibility of crashing in through the gates. It appeared to be impossible without a tank or dynamite. They discussed the legality. They had heard about this place. Who hadn't? Private. Inviolate. Better report back to the Jungle Patrol. Let them handle it.

Yes, word had gotten around about Killer's Town. In the

prisons, in the underworld, in the police bureaus, and especially in Bangalla's capital of Mawitaan. The news had as yet failed to reach in one direction—into the interior, to the jungle tribes, and beyond that to the mysterious Deep Woods. In that forbidden place, guarded by taboo and the deadly poison weapons of the pygmy Bandar, behind the hidden entrance under the roaring waterfall, word had not yet reached the fabulous skull throne of the Phantom, the Ghost Who Walks. Busied with internal problems involving the peace of the jungle—the arrogant and powerful princes of the Misty Mountains; the rampaging Tirangi, returning periodically to their head-hunting raids—all this and more occupied the legendary figure loved by jungle folk, but hated and feared by evildoers everywhere. So far, Killer's Town had escaped the notice of the Phantom. That would not last for long.

CHAPTER 6

Following the jailbreak, a Citizen's Council was formed by the black Lord Mayor of Mawitaan, Ito Togando, a cousin of Police Chief Togando. The Council included the Police Chief, Colonel Weeks of the Jungle Patrol, General Sago Togando who was commander of Bangalla's weak little army and a cousin of Ito, the publisher of the Mawitaan Daily, Gando Togando, cousin of Sago, Chief Justice Amy Togando, cousin of Gando, the chairman of the Bangalla Bank, Okan Togando, cousin of Amu, and several other civic leaders. They had a heated discussion.

What could they do about the pest hole on their border, known as Killer's Town? "Den of iniquity," "infested with criminals," "intolerable menace," "rats' nest," "vile cancer," were some of the printable expressions used. Much more was unprintable. "What are the police doing about this criminal haven?" demanded the Lord Mayor. The Chief spread his arms wide, indicating helplessness, and asked Colonel Weeks to explain the situation. He did. The Patrol's legal department had looked into it. Killer's Town, originally a royal grant from a king, long dead, was an independent sovereignty, an enclave like Monaco or Vatican City. One Matthew Crumb had owned it, until he sold it to Percival Koy.

"This is ridiculous," roared General Sago Togando. "My army can storm that place and wipe it off the map in a few hours."

"Quite possibly," said Colonel Weeks, "but that would be

illegal."

"Who cares? We know what the place is. Nobody would miss it," said the Lord Mayor, and the cousins agreed. Weeks shook his head.

"Quite true, but we are faced with the ancient dilemma. Does the end justify the means? Shall we break the law to destroy lawbreakers? Shall we commit a crime to catch criminals?" he asked. The cousins looked to the Chief Justice. The sage man nodded.

"He is right. We are the law. We cannot break the law on the pretext of enforcing it."

"Then what can we do?" was the question, followed by a thoughtful silence.

"First, this is a matter of international law. We are not experts," said Colonel Weeks. "We can appeal to the World Court or the United Nations for a ruling."

"That will take forever," said the Lord Mayor.

"It will take a long time," agreed Weeks. "In the meantime, the Jungle Patrol will keep the place under round- the-clock surveillance. We will try to prevent more criminals from entering or leaving."

"A few sticks of dynamite would do the job quicker and better," growled General Sago Togando.

So it was decided. Let the Jungle Patrol handle it. For the time being, that would satisfy the press and public opinion. As in all government matters, the important thing was to give the impression that something was being done.

The Patrol began their round-the-clock watch, with four vehicles on four sides of the town, two patrolmen in each car, on eight-hour shifts. Twenty-four men in all, a drain on the small, tightly organized Patrol. They positioned themselves close enough to watch the walls and gate of Killer's Town. They were spotted at once. A loud voice from a megaphone warned them to take off. They remained. Standing on the roof of the Killer Hilton, Koy shouted a last warning. The patrolmen consulted each other by radio, then sat tight The firing began. High-powered bullets hit within inches of the vehicles. The misses were deliberate. But they might not remain misses. The officer in charge, Sergeant Dave Hill, radioed headquarters.

"They're firing on us. Can we fire back?" he asked.

"No. Pull further back," ordered Colonel Weeks.

The vehicles retreated a quarter mile. The barrage continued. A few bullets nicked the cars. The vehicles retreated again out of gunshot range. But at this distance, their observation was also limited, as was their ability to stop men from entering and leaving. They continued to watch through binoculars, cursing that long-dead king who had created his free port in the first place.

Inside, Koy and his men were jubilant. In their first encounter with the law, they had made the Patrol back up and eat crow. With the hated memory of Colonel Weeks still fresh, Koy was especially glad it was the Patrol being humiliated.

A tattered figure wandered about during the barrage, at first rushing for cover under a porch, then watching, puzzled. Matthew Crumb, with his inevitable can of beer, was tolerated by Killer's Town as a sort of village idiot. He went from building to building at will, watching construction, watching the strange violent men arrive. None seemed to leave. He hung around the bars, cadging drinks, watching the gambling in the day and night casino, marveling at the scantily dressed, highly decorated "ladies" who had become a permanent fixture, and wondering occasionally, dimly, what he had done on that day when he had so casually sold New Metropolis. He'd been granted a cot in the cellar of the hotel, but he still hadn't been paid. Eagle, now a busy man, was hard to find, harder to talk to. He would dismiss Matthew with a pat on the back, a chit for a free beer at the bar, or a kick when he was in a hurry. Matthew was a law-abiding man, more or less, and he was disturbed when he began to realize what kind of people these were. He was more disturbed when he saw the Jungle Patrol fired on. He had always admired those brisk young men, and in his youth had once tried to join them, but failed to qualify. Ah, well, he thought as he shambled back to his cot in the cellar for a nap, what's done is done.

The Patrol continued to observe from a distance, attempting to quarantine the town. But they were spread too thin, too far apart. An army would be needed to surround the place properly. Men were able to enter or leave at night without trouble, knowing the positions of the vehicles. And there was nothing to be done about the big amphibian planes that roared in and out during the night several times a week to and from parts unknown. So the population swelled, and Koy's safe bulged, but the presence of those Patrolmen out there still annoyed him. From the roof of his hotel, he would occasionally fire a rifle bullet, just to annoy them. The patrolmen ducked, gritted their teeth, and waited. This assignment was the most hated of all. To watch that crowd of gangsters and killers, to hear their laughter, shouts, curses, fights; to hear the shrill voices of their 'ladies'—so close, yet unable to do anything about it. It was frustrating, aggravating, irritating, monstrous!

Colonel Weeks suffered in silence with his men. The Jungle Patrol is an elite corps, proud of two hundred fifty years of tradition, dedicated to incorruptible service, jealous of its unblemished reputation. To be mocked and derided by these vicious criminals was almost more than these proud young men and their Colonel could bear. More than once, law or no law, they were ready to charge into that snake pit. Killer's Town, with guns blazing. After all, one patrolman can handle ten criminals. But they restrained themselves, hung on, and, like their Colonel, suffered in silence. Someday, they told themselves. Someday.

CHAPTER 7

Caroline Weeks, the Colonel's beautiful, red-haired, eighteen-year-old daughter, stepped off the big plane at Mawitaan airport and ran into her father's waiting arms. He had not seen her for four years. A widower. Weeks had sent her to England to live with his sister and go to school there. Her trips to Bangalla were not frequent, because it was a long distance and expensive, and jungle patrolmen, even the Colonel, receive a great deal of respect, honor, and glory, but not much money. At Caroline's age, four years make a huge difference. She had left him, a gangling, freckled, awkward child. It took him a moment to realize that the red-haired beauty who leaped into his arms was his little Caroline. Now she would spend the entire summer vacation with him before returning to the university. They would have a chance to become reacquainted.

Caroline, in those years away, remembered her father as a sharp but gentle and authoritative figure, the heroic leader of a band of heroes. Returning, she wondered if her memory was false. She was afraid of disappointment in seeing him with older eyes. But she was delighted to find that her father was as alert, gentle, and strong as she had remembered. And after the first few days, he found that the red- haired young beauty called Caroline was still half-tomboy, still produced freckles after an hour in the sun, still laughed and rolled on the lawn with her old dog Shep, still loved horseback riding and tennis, still loved to sit on his lap occasionally and hear about her mother and the old days of the Patrol. It was a happy reunion, and half the Jungle Patrol fell madly in love with her. They were all dismayed to learn that she had a young man back in England.

Weeks had put his daughter on a horse for the first time when she was five years old. She had ridden ever since. She was an expert horsewoman, excelling at jumping, racing, and the difficult art of dressage. As soon as she had caught her breath, unpacked, said hello to everyone, and spent a few days reviving old memories of the town where she had spent her childhood, she went to the stables.

Though the Patrol was motorized, they still kept a dozen fine riding horses, plus a gentle little mare that the older wives could ride. They brought out the mare for Caroline. She laughed and petted the gentle beast, then picked a spirited brown stallion. The stablemaster wasn't sure about letting her have Dynamite. Too much to handle. But Caroline put Dynamite through his paces, jumped him over a few fences, raced him around the field, and returned to the applause of the stablemaster, stableboys, and half the watching Patrol, including the Colonel. After that, Caroline rode every day on trails she had known since she was a child. It never occurred to anyone that she would ride as far out as the Phantom Trail. No one told her about Killer's Town. Maybe they forgot because of wanting to forget that frustrating place.

It was a beautiful morning and Dynamite moved like the wind. People stared and waved as the Colonel's daughter raced by in jodhpurs, riding boots, and an orange-red shirt that matched her own red mane flowing behind her. Soon she had left the dirt road at the edge of town and moved onto the loamy shadowy path that led into the jungle. This, for some reason, had always been called the Phantom Trail. She wondered about the name, telling herself to ask about the origins of it when she got home.

In England, she had dreamed about this jungle. The path seemed wider and bumpier and more used than she remembered. Trees were occasionally scarred and bushes bent back and broken, as though a large truck had passed. She noticed a tire track in the dust. Like everywhere else, she supposed things had progressed a bit there, too. But beyond these few signs, it seemed unchanged. As she rode deeper into the jungle, there were monkeys in the trees chattering at her, the whirr of wings as brightly colored birds took off, bright eyes gleaming from the bushes, then a soft scampering as small furry animals hurried away, all startled by the hooves of Dynamite. She went on like this, walking, trotting, galloping, stopping, then walking again, for two or three hours. She suddenly realized that she was far from home, that she was hungry, and would never get back in time for lunch with her father. There was a road sign ahead. She approached it and paused for a moment. "*Killer's Town—Private—No Admittance.*"

Some sort of joke? What else could it be? There had never been a town out here. Caroline had a wild sense of humor, and she enjoyed it in other people. She wondered who had made that official-looking sign. Some mad person she'd love to meet, she thought. She rode on, around the bend, again feeling her hunger, thinking she should have brought a sandwich, thinking she should turn back now, but intrigued by the sign, and not wanting to stop. Then miraculously, high walls appeared before her, shining white buildings behind them, gleaming glass, paved streets seen through the tall iron-barred fence. Wonderful! New suburbs were springing up everywhere. This one had been built while she was away.

She rode up to the closed gate. A man had seen her coming. As she approached and he saw her clearly, he put his rifle aside and unlocked the gate.

"Do you have a restaurant or cafe here? I'd love tea and a sandwich," she said.

He grinned at her. Another 'lady' for the town.

"Sure thing," he said. "Come right in."

As she entered the gateway, she was aware of the distant autohorns honking. She noticed that the man made a face toward the direction of that sound, wondered about that, then rode on. The gates closed behind her. The man watched her appreciatively. Not like the others who came here. This one was young and looked like a real lady . . . hard to tell them these days. He wondered what lucky man would get this one. Why wonder? Koy, naturally. And a mile away on a shaded hill, the watching patrolmen lowered their binoculars and stared at each other in amazement

"Could that be Caroline Weeks? Or was it someone who looked like her?"

"Someone who looked like her. What would Caroline be doing out here?"

"Right. She must be"—he looked at his watch—"having lunch with the old man right now."

"Right. But–"

"But what?"

"That horse. It looked like Dynamite."

"Lots of brown horses look like Dynamite."

"Let's call in anyhow, to make sure."

"Right."

They reached the Patrol headquarters radio room. "Everything lousy as usual out there?" said the cheery voice of the H. Q. operator.

"As usual. Say, do you happen to know—is Miss Weeks having lunch with the Colonel?"

"Now what business is that of yours, bub?"

"Put it down to unrequited love."

"We're in the same club, bub. Nope, the beauteous lady took off on her brown charger this a.m. I saw her go. Wished I was going too."

The two patrolmen looked at each other in alarm.

"Find out if she's back yet."

"Why bub?"

"No questions. Please, just make it fast. Urgent."

"Urgent? Er, sure."

They waited in their vehicle on top of the shaded hill, a mile from Killer's Town. Then the radio broke in.

"This is Colonel Weeks. Sergeant Hill?"

"Yes sir."

"Why are you asking about my daughter."

Sergeant Hill gulped, looked at his partner, then plunged in.

"I don't wish to alarm you, sir. Maybe it wasn't Miss Weeks at all."

"What wasn't? Come to the point, Hill."

"We watched a red-haired girl in a red shirt ride a brown horse into Killer's Town a few minutes ago, sir."

"Killer's Town. Who was it?"

"We're a mile away, sir, as you know. We were both watching through binoculars."

"How could you imagine it was—she was—my daughter?"

"It's stupid, sir, but we both got the same idea."

"Was the woman taken in by force, Hill?"

"No sir. Rode up by herself, went in by herself. No force."

"My god!" A silence. Then, "Can't be. I'll send out men to find her. Keep in touch. Over."

The men went out. Naturally, they didn't find her. But they did talk to people who'd seen her racing by, entering the Phantom Trail. The men, patrolmen trained in tracking, followed the hoofprints of Dynamite all the way to the sign: "*Killer's Town—Private—No Admittance.*"

CHAPTER 8

A s Caroline rode into the town, she was surprised by the empty streets. It should be buzzing with people at midday. She couldn't know that the inhabitants of Killer's Town caroused all night and slept half the day. Most of them were just now having breakfast. There were a few native workmen sitting in the shade eating a simple lunch. One man walked out on the street, an old barefooted man with a scraggly beard and ragged clothes, carrying a can of beer. Caroline reined up the tired Dynamite beside him.

"Sir, where can I go for a sandwich and tea?"

He shaded his eyes and looked up at her. Ages had passed since anyone called him sir.

"The inn over there, I guess," he said.

"Thank you, sir."

She rode off. He shook his head. He knew a lady when he saw one. Such a fresh, lovely young woman. What was she doing here? Caroline rode to the middle of the block, to the big white building set back from the street, fronted by a broad green lawn. She giggled at the sign: Killer Hilton. She dismounted, tied Dynamite to a gatepost, and walked into the inn. It seemed an odd hotel, no bellboys, no desk clerks, no front desk. In fact, no one but a tall thin man who looked at her curiously and, in answer to her query about food, pointed to a side door.

She entered a room that was filled with laughing and shouting men and a few women. It appeared to be a bar and grill, more bar than grill. The room quieted as all turned to look at her. She was used to men's stares, but not like this. She had the sudden feeling that she'd walked into a den of wild animals. She turned to leave. A young man walked up to her, and took her arm. He had curly blond hair and pale-blue eyes, like a wolf.

"Help you, Miss?" he said, grinning.

"I just wanted a sandwich and some tea," said Caroline, pulling her arm away.

The blond man turned to the others.

"She just wants a sandwich and tea," he said, trying to imitate Caroline's prim British accent. Everyone howled with laughter.

"I'll fix you up—and I mean fix," he added loudly for the others. This caused more laughter and shouting. Caroline was frightened now. She tried to pull away, but the man held her tightly and started to lead her to a side door. Two other men had come in another door, Slim and Koy. Slim was pointing to the girl.

"Just a minute," said Koy, walking toward Caroline and Pretty.

"I saw her first," said Pretty.

"Who are you? How did you get here?" said Koy, ignoring Pretty.

"I was out riding. I just saw this place. I came in for lunch," said Caroline, bewildered now as well as frightened. "Just saw the place. Do you know what place this is?"

"No. I saw a silly—I mean an odd—sign on the road."

"Silly? Odd?" said Koy, grinning at the girl's obvious confusion, as he took inventory of her clear skin and youthful figure. "Come with me into my office, and we'll discuss this."

"I saw her first," said Pretty.

"There's nothing to discuss," said Caroline, becoming angry. "I've done nothing. I wish to leave."

Koy grinned again, still ignoring Pretty.

"How do I know you're not a spy?"

"A spy! For what?" she said indignantly. "My name is Caroline Weeks. My father is Colonel Weeks of the Jungle Patrol."

A bomb dropped in the middle of the room might have caused the same surprise. The men and women at the tables stared. Even Pretty reacted with a backward step. But Killer Koy grabbed her arm and pulled her to him so that his eyes glared into hers.

"You're who? Are you putting me on?"

"Caroline Weeks," said Caroline weakly.

"Your father's who?"

"Colonel Weeks."

"I thought you said that."

He stepped back and surveyed her from head to toe.

"How about that! You just dropped in for tea and toast."

"No, for a sandwich," said Caroline unhappily, aware that something was terribly wrong.

"Does your daddy know you're here?" continued Koy, while the crowd listened alertly.

"No. He knows I took a ride into the jungle."

"Knows you took a ride. Didn't he tell you about this place?"

"This place . . . uh . . . no, what place?"

"Killer's Town."

"Is that a real name?"

The crowd laughed at that, a quick, ugly laugh.

Koy looked at the girl thoughtfully. He couldn't believe his luck. The one man he'd met in this new world whom he thoroughly hated was Colonel Weeks. And this was his daughter who had just walked in. He waved to Sport, standing at the side with squat, powerful Baldy.

"Lock her up in that room next to my office," he said.

Pretty stepped up to Koy, his pale-blue eyes narrow.

"I told you, I saw her first."

Killer Koy looked at him thoughtfully. This mad dog was bound to cause trouble, unless he knew who was giving the orders. He smiled for a moment. Pretty relaxed. Then Killer Koy slammed him in the mouth. As Pretty staggered back, Sport chopped him on the back of his neck, and Baldy kicked him in the stomach as he fell. He lay on the floor, clutching his stomach and writhing. Baldy was ready with another kick to the head, but Koy stopped him.

"Any more trouble from you, and you're stone dead. Got that, 'Pretty boy'?" he snarled.

Pretty groaned. Koy kicked him in the side.

"Got that?"

"Yes."

"Throw him outside till he cools off," said Koy. Sport and Baldy did just that. They tossed Pretty from the veranda to the grass. Pretty lay there, curled up, his head filled with murder. When the time comes, when I get my chance, he told himself.

Koy talked quickly to his little group of aides. "Keep an eye on that guy all the time. If he acts up again, blow his head off."

Caroline, pressed back against the wall, watched the action in horror. What kind of place was this? Who were these awful men? Nobody told her. Koy's orders were carried out, and she was locked up in a small bare room on the top floor of the inn—a room without windows.

Colonel Weeks, desperately anxious, waited in his office until night. Though the hoofprints could have been Dynamite's, though the red-haired girl might have been Caroline, she could have been someone else. He tried to recall if he had mentioned Killer's Town to her. He couldn't remember for certain, but he had a sinking feeling he hadn't. Why would she enter the place? If she was ignorant of the place, could she have gone in out of curiosity. Why? He tortured himself, waiting, wondering, hoping that his precious daughter would come bouncing into his office, telling about her great day on Dynamite, and all this worry would be for nothing. The entire Patrol was worrying with him. The new off-duty men watched from the windows or the gates. The word spread to the far-flung patrolmen on missions—and they kept in touch by radio. "Has the girl returned yet?"

"No." Tension mounted each hour. As it was reaching the snapping point—it snapped.

A note for Colonel Weeks was on its way from Killer's Town. One of the native workmen had come out of the gates waving a white handkerchief on a stick. Obviously scared, he had walked directly to one of the Jungle Patrol observation vehicles. The man had been forced to do this. His wife, who worked as a cleaning woman in the Inn, was held as hostage to guarantee his behavior. Koy watched him approach the Patrol car through binoculars, pleased with his own cleverness. The Patrol car raced back to town with the man, sending the word ahead by radio. Weeks waited nervously at the front gate, pacing back and forth until the car arrived. He snatched the note from the frightened man.

Weeks:
She's here. Want to make a deal to get her out? Drive back with this man to our gates. Come alone, or you'll never see her alive.

The note was unsigned. Weeks ordered the patrolmen out of the car and took the wheel. The trembling black man sat beside him. A group of patrolmen massed around the car, protesting.

"You can't go alone."

"I've no choice."

He was wearing no jacket, no hat, no gun, as he backed the car out of the Patrol driveway and sped off into the night. The patrolmen stared after him, angry, helpless. He raced through the town, out to the Phantom Trail, and sped on grimly through the woods, disregarding the bumps. The black man held on as the car bounced.

"Did you see my daughter?" asked the Colonel.

"No sir."

That was the extent of the conversation. The Patrol cars still posted about Killer's Town saw the lights of the car as it approached. They had been forewarned by radio and did not interfere. The Colonel sped past the road sign—Killer's Town—then stopped at the closed gates. There were no lights on in the town behind the wall and also no sounds. They were waiting. The Colonel jumped from his car and ran to the gate. He grabbed the bars, shaking them, and called out.

"I'm here."

Brilliant light flashed into his eyes, temporarily blinding him. A dozen powerful searchlights were trained on the gate. He covered his eyes with his arm. A voice boomed out, amplified by a megaphone.

"You got my note, Weeks."

"Where's my daughter?" Weeks shouted, still covering his eyes.

"She's with us. Safe—not hurt yet."

Weeks groaned at that.

"Want her back? Here's the deal. Get off our backs. Get your guys away from my town for good. We want your promise in writing. We want those Boy Scouts of yours out of those hills and gone for good. Got it?"

"Listen to me, you miserable . . . if you think," began Weeks, boiling with fury.

"Easy, pop. We're holding all the cards—your kid."

Weeks doubled his fists, trying to control his anger, and shouted through clenched teeth.

"How do I know she's safe and unhurt as you say?"

"Don't you trust our word?" came the mocking reply.

"No!"

"Okay, wait a minute." Then some indistinct mumbling. Weeks waited tensely, still blinded by the bright lights. Suddenly, he was in the dark. Another searchlight turned on, shining not at him but at the roof level of the high building called Killer Hilton.

On top of the renovated old building that had formerly been the Governor-General's mansion, there was a railing and platform, the kind known as a widow's walk. Two searchlights illuminated it. Several figures appeared up there, a girl held by two burly men. In the dark, outside the gates, Weeks stared. Caroline's voice came through the megaphone.

"I'm—I'm alright, daddy," she said.

"Caroline, have they hurt you?" shouted Weeks.

"No, daddy," came the slight, frightened voice.

Evidently the megaphone switched hands. The next voice was the first one he had heard.

"No, daddy," the voice mocked. "Not yet," it added.

The widow's walk was suddenly dark, then searchlights once more blazed into Weeks's eyes.

"Okay pop, that's it. You know the deal. Get rid of those snoopers. Those Boy Scouts. I want them gone—by dawn! Think it over. Now, blow!"

The lights went out. There was ribald laughter from the town.

Back in her little room, Caroline heard it. She had heard it all. She pictured her father out there beyond the gates. What a fool I was to ride into this place, she told herself again, for the tenth or twentieth time. "Poor daddy," she sobbed aloud.

Weeks drove back alone, slowly. Everything he loved and believed in was at stake. His child, the Patrol, his honor. How could he bow to this blackmail? The morale of the Patrol would disintegrate. His own private moral standards could not allow it. Yet he had to think of Caroline. He reached headquarters, and went directly to his office, ignoring the waiting patrolmen. There, not a drinking man, he downed two slugs of whiskey, then called Chief Togando. News had reached the police chief and he got to Weeks's side in ten minutes. Togando had never seen his old friend so gray and broken.

"That hood's got my little girl," he said.

Togando nodded and touched his shoulder.

"You got a note?"

Weeks showed it to him, and then, with some effort, pulled himself together and told about the incident at the gate.

"Isn't there some legal way we can get into that place?" asked Togando angrily.

"We've been through all that. None that we know of yet. And certainly not now, with Caroline in there."

"We might talk to Sago," said the Chief.

"Your cousin, the General? No, he'd be all out for a frontal attack. How I'd love to see that," said Weeks bitterly. "What can I do, Mano? I can't give in to blackmail." It was the first time he'd ever called the Chief by his first name.

"I don't know, Randolph. We keep going around the bush."

"But now Caroline's in the bush," said Weeks tensely.

"We'll think of something. Meanwhile, we'll keep this to ourselves. Don't let it out."

Weeks nodded. The Chief got up, patted Weeks on the back, and left.

Give it time? Think of something? What was there to think about? Police, army, navy—none could help; none had the authority.

Exhausted, he lay forward on his arms on his desk and fell asleep.

Dawn at Killer's Town. From the widow's walk atop the inn, Koy, Eagle, and Sport peered through binoculars. In the distance, at four points of the compass, the Jungle Patrol cars were holding their observation posts. Koy swore.

"What'll we do now? That idiot Colonel hasn't moved."

"Give it an hour," said Eagle.

Koy agreed. They left the roof for breakfast—a raw egg in whiskey was Koy's usual meal. They discussed the next step if the Patrol cars did not pull out. There were several ideas, then Eagle the lawyer came up with a good one, something he had seen in an old building on the grounds. Koy chuckled approvingly. The hour passed. Returning to the roof, they could see that the Patrol cars were still there. Koy nodded with a cruel grin.

"Do it," he said.

About an hour later, Colonel Weeks was awakened by the telephone on his desk. It was a direct report for him from one of the Patrol cars at the site of Killer's Town. What the Colonel heard made his eyes smolder with fury.

A cage had been put up on the side of the inn, hanging from the roof, near the sign: Killer Hilton. Inside the cage was a figure, a girl. Caroline Weeks, alive and weeping. Weeks slammed the phone back on the receiver. He looked about wildly, then rushed to the rifle rack on the wall. If the Patrol, police, army, and navy were helpless, he wasn't, he assured himself. Two patrolmen burst into the room as he pulled the rifle from the rack. Despite his angry commands, they forcibly led him back to his desk. He glared at them.

"They've got Caroline in a cage!" he shouted.

They nodded. They'd heard the report.

"They want our men taken away. But that won't end it. Then they'll want something else. That's the way it is with blackmailers," he said brokenly. The patrolmen stood silently, watching their leader wrestle with himself.

"But she's in that cage. Those rats won't stop at anything — they know we're helpless." He suddenly stopped and stared at the men, then slapped his hands together.

"I want to be alone," he said.

"Colonel, are you sure----?"

"Don't worry. I won't do anything foolish."

The men left the office. Weeks grabbed his phone. "Why didn't I think of him at once?" he told himself. Then, into the phone. "Radio, put me on the X band at once."

What if he wasn't there? He could be anywhere. Waiting for

the call to go through. Weeks kept his fingers crossed. He had to be there.

Excitement erupted in the Patrol radio room. The X band was the only contact with the Jungle Patrol's unknown Commander, the figure at the top of the Patrol organization chart. There was an office next to the Colonel's. On the door was the lettering: "Office of the Commander." The door was always locked. Only one man had the key. Colonel Weeks. The few who had peeked inside this office, when the Colonel went in, described it as a bare room—no ' windows, no furniture, no rug, only a heavy iron safe set into the wooden floor. Inside this safe, in some unknown way, orders from the Commander appeared. Their arrival was signaled by a light outside the door. When the Colonel opened the safe—he alone had the combination, there was a note, always brief and to the point, seemingly materialized out of thin air. Replies back to the Commander were also placed in the safe, where after a time they vanished.

There were also other ways to reach the Commander: by radio, by mail through a post-office box under the name Walker, by homing pigeons at cotes at the jungle's edge, or by the swift falcon, Fraka, also kept at the cote. Radio was the swiftest, and now Colonel Weeks waited at his phone impatiently. Maybe the Commander wouldn't be there, wherever there was. No one knew where the Commander's transmitter was. Somewhere . . . out there. There had been a Commander ever since the Patrol was founded two hundred fifty years ago. He had always, it seemed, remained anonymous. Patrolmen speculated. Was he one man or many? Why was he unknown? Who was he—or they? There were never any answers.

Now, the Colonel's phone rang. He grabbed it anxiously.

"Hello, Colonel Weeks here," he said.

A voice replied, deep, pleasant, but with the ring of immense authority, the voice he had heard many times, of a man he'd never seen.

"This is the Commander. How are you, Colonel Weeks? What can I do for you?"

CHAPTER 9

The man speaking, and the place where his voice was coming from, was far stranger than anything any of the patrolmen had ever imagined when they discussed the mystery of their unknown Commander. At the eastern end of the jungle, near the remote Misty Mountains, was a place all jungle folk knew as the Deep Woods. No one in the Patrol had even heard of it. And though few had even been close to it, and only a handful had actually seen it through the centuries, all jungle folk knew it was taboo. Even the fierce Tirangi, on their occasional relapses into headhunting, avoided it as did the primitive Massagni, rumored to be cannibals in this age of moonwalks. The Deep Woods was feared and avoided for several reasons. This was the land of the pygmy Bandar, whose poison weapons caused instant death. The pygmies, it was well known, treasured the privacy of their shadowy domain and resented intruders. Then, too, even if you were foolish enough to go looking for them, the Deep Woods were hard to find. You never knew you were there, until a pygmy peered out of the bushes, with a poison arrow in his tiny bow. There was one clue, the sound of a roaring waterfall. When you heard that, if you were wise and not bent on suicide, you turned around and ran in the opposite direction.

But the real taboo concerning the Deep Woods was another more mysterious matter. Somewhere behind the waterfall, reached by secret entrances, were the fabulous Skull Throne and Skull Cave, the legendary home of the Phantom, the Ghost Who Walks, the Man Who Cannot Die.

At this moment if you were there, you might see a large animal resembling a dog enter the cave. The mouth of the cave, carved by the wind and water of eons, looks like a giant skull. And the animal that looks like a dog is actually a big mountain wolf with the pale-blue eyes of his kind. He trots through the cave, past rocky chambers containing a variety of wonders: a dim grotto containing rows of engraved stone plaques behind which are the vaults of long-dead Phantoms—twenty generations of them. Another chamber contains shelves filled with large folio volumes, the chronicles of the Phantom. Another chamber glitters and gleams in the torchlight, filled with treasure chests brimming over with precious jewels, gold, silver, and platinum objects. A deep, pleasant voice comes from another chamber and the wolf heads for that. Inside is a powerful radio transmitter. Seated, speaking and listening, is a large man clad in tights, hooded and masked, with two guns in holsters on a gunbelt that bears his ancient insignia, the Sign of the Skull.

"Your daughter, Colonel Weeks? Killer's Town. I've just returned to Bangalla from a distant place and know nothing of this. Tell me."

This is the voice on the other end of the X band. The unknown Commander of the Jungle Patrol.

Colonel Weeks told him all about it—Killer Koy and the new town, the impotency of the Jungle Patrol and all other enforcement agencies, his night trip to the gates; the ultimatum from Killer Koy. Then of Caroline in the cage.

"Have you told me everything?" asked the Phantom.

"All that we know. The Lower Gamma bank gang are there. Also the escaped lifers from here. But the plane goes in and out several times a week. Perhaps there are many more criminals."

"What happened to the old man who owned the place?"

"Matthew Crumb? We heard he's still there, unless they've killed him," said the Colonel. He waited for a moment.

"I will look into the matter, Colonel."

"What shall we do?"

"Nothing, Colonel, until you hear from me. Over and out."

There was a click and that was all. Colonel Weeks stared at the phone. Do nothing? How could he do that with Caroline in that cage? But what else could he do? Orders are orders.

Guran the pygmy chief, and a dozen other little Bandar warriors were waiting at the Skull Throne as the Phantom dashed out of the Skull Cave with Devil, the wolf, at his heels. They were waiting for him to start the feast spread on mats on the ground before the throne, celebrating the Phantom's return from a distant mission. But he had no time for a feast now. He raced to a patch of grass where Hero, the big white stallion, was grazing, untied, and quickly saddled him. As he did, he explained to Guran the nature and location of the place where he was headed. Guran and the others pleaded with him to eat before leaving. They knew he was hungry. He glanced at the feast, sighed, but shook his head, then leaped upon Hero. As he wheeled the great steed about, he swung low off the saddle, grabbed a roasted fowl from the mat, then raced off. The pygmies laughed and cheered, as he disappeared behind the roaring waterfall, pursued by Devil.

The jungle does not have planes, trains, superhighways, or even roads. Only thickly overgrown paths. But there is one way to move fast. The Phantom on Hero sped through the jungle, leaping over bushes and logs where no path existed, and reached the bank of a swift, foaming mountain stream. A drum message from the Deep Woods had preceded him, so that a large raft was waiting for him with two Mori raftsmen. They were of the Mori fisher folk, the most expert of jungle people in the skills of the sea and streams. The two men, wearing only loin cloths, smiled at the sight of their big masked friend. The Phantom dismounted, shook their hands, then led Hero and Devil onto the raft. Without further ado, the Mori untied the raft and, wielding their nine-foot poles, pushed the raft into the channel of the stream.

This was icy water from the Misty Mountains. The grade here was steep, and the stream roared and foamed as it raced toward the distant sea, carrying the raft with it. It was a wild, bumpy ride. Devil, the wolf, remained in a crouch to keep his balance. The Phantom held tightly to Hero's reins as the stallion braced himself. The raft pitched and rolled, bounced over rocks, leaped through the air over low waterfalls, landing with a crash; rumbled over rapids, drenching men and animals in the icy spray. After three hours of this, the pace lessened, as the mountain torrent widened into a calm river nearing the sea. The Mori poled the raft to the bank. Another handshake and the Phantom, Hero, and Devil leaped onto the bank and were gone.

The Mori watched until they were out of sight. Usually their big friend joked with them, and was easy and relaxed. This time, he was grim and in a hurry, headed for some trouble he hadn't explained. Whoever was causing the trouble would wish they hadn't, now that the Phantom was on the way, the Mori told each other as they poled out into the stream.

From the top of a high tree that grew only a hundred feet from the wall, the Phantom could look into Killer's Town. He saw a few men walking idly in the streets. He noted the guard at the gate, and guards patrolling inside the wall. And he could see the cage hanging by the inn sign, with the girl sitting inside. It appeared to be an old tiger cage, used by some long-gone animal dealer. Several men stopped beneath the cage and called up to her, but he was too far away to hear their words. He could hear their laughter as they walked on into the inn, and he saw her cover her face with her hands. On the other side of the town, he could see the wharf on the salt-water inlet. A speedboat had pulled up, discharging several men with boxes.

The Phantom climbed down, and made his way quickly through the bushes, around the town, getting close to the wharf. As he waited, a big amphibian plane roared down from the sky and made a smooth landing near the wharf. Several men rushed out to meet the plane and its passengers. The Phantom, crouched under bushes, was close enough to hear them.

"Killer, this here's Pug and Ossie. Broke out of a limey pen. Plenty of lettuce. Want room and board."

"Sure. We're expecting you boys. Rooms ready. Five hundred a night. Pay at the desk," said Killer.

"Five hundred? The bloke told us three," protested one of the arrivals.

"Ain't you heard of inflation? Everything's gone up," said the one called Killer. They all laughed, but without enjoyment.

"We also want to see your heist," continued Killer, pointing to a suitcase one man was carrying. "Diamonds, wasn't it?"

"That's our business," said the man.

"Also ours. We want a cut. That's part of the rent."

The two arrivals turned angrily on the third man.

"You didn't tell us about that, Eagle."

The skinny man shrugged.

"Killer makes the rules."

"Take it or leave it," said Killer. "If you know a better place, go to it."

The men stared at each other. One of the arrivals made a move toward his coat. The other one grabbed his arm.

"If that's a gun, park it at the desk," said Killer calmly.

"Nobody carries rods, except us," he said, pointing upward. The men looked up. A guard was on the roof of the wharf warehouse, pointing a rifle at them.

"Okay?" said Killer.

"Okay," said the man.

"That's the inn. Wait in my office," said Killer. The two men from the "limey pen" walked away, talking angrily to each other. \
Killer grinned at the man with him.

"Anything else, Eagle?"

"Sharp sent this with Pilot, for storage. From Hong Kong—half million in snow."

Killer whistled.

"Wow," he said, as they walked off.

I've seen enough, the Phantom told himself, as he crawled away through the bushes. That scene, plus the story from the Colonel on the phone, gave him a good picture of Killer's Town. Well named—a den of thieves and murderers. As for that poor girl in the cage, she was the first priority. He moved a half mile down the beach, through thickets and swamp, to reach a concealed clearing where he'd left Hero and Devil. He untied the pack roll behind the saddle, took out clothes and dressed—trousers, topcoat, sunglasses, scarf, hat—completely concealing his costume. Then petting his animals and giving them a command to wait, he returned to the wharf. He climbed a tall tree and waited.

There was a small gate here with an armed guard. A man left the amphibian plane tied to the dock and walked to the gate.

"Hi, Pilot," the guard greeted him.

"Hi."

There were happy little screams from inside as two young women rushed up to embrace Pilot, evidently a favorite. He embraced both of them. Then they lit cigarettes and talked excitedly. At the same time, the Phantom climbed out on a branch, then swung over the wall, avoiding the spikes and broken glass atop it, and landed lightly on the other side. He looked about quickly. No one had noticed him. Then he walked casually to the center of the town.

The two new arrivals, the "limeys", were standing beneath the cage with a third man.

"Hey, look at her. Who's she for?"

"Skip it, Ossie. Part of a special deal of the chiefs."

"Chief?"

"Killer Koy."

The one called Ossie called an obscenity to the girl in the cage. The men laughed and went into the bar. The girl buried her face in her hands. "Will this nightmare ever end?" she asked herself, for the tenth or twentieth time. "I've got to be strong, I won't cry," she told herself as tears brimmed in her eyes. Two other men wandered out of the bar and looked up at the red-haired girl in her flaming silk shirt and riding pants. One of them called an obscene comment Caroline gritted her teeth, then yelled down at them.

"You filthy beasts. You're horrible, horrible."

"Who's filthy? I just had a bath."

A few other men peered out of the swinging doors. All laughed.

"The Colonel's daughter, how about that?" said Killer Koy.

"Killer, what a deal you've got here. No law, no fuzz— and the Colonel's daughter. What you going to do with her?"

"Keeping her in storage for a while."

"For who?"

"For me. Who else, stupid?"

"Hey, sweetheart, any room up there for me?" shouted one of the men at the bar doors. And he made an obscene joke that caused a roar of laughter from the others, Killer laughing loudest of all.

"You can say that again," he said as they all went into the barroom, laughing.

Caroline sat rigidly.

"I've got to control myself. They treat me like I'm a monkey in the zoo. But I've got to ignore them—I—" Then she was shaking with a fit of sobbing.

A voice came to her from the street below.

"Courage, Caroline."

She looked down through tear-dimmed eyes, then wiped her eyes. A man wearing a hat and coat had just gone into the bar. Was that the one? Something good about that voice, friendly and good. Was there hope, or had she imagined it? She stared down into the street.

In a town of strangers, a man can remain unnoticed for a while. The man in the hat and coat, the Phantom, walked casually through the bar. The men there were drinking, in intimate conversation with the women, or had their heads together, plotting future deals. A few glanced at the passerby with little interest. He went on into the casino where men were crowded around the two dice tables. A few were at blackjack and roulette. The dice players were not quiet bettors. The place was bedlam, curses of happiness or despair as they won or lost. The passer-by, a stranger among strangers, moved on, leaving the casino. It was dark outside now, and he wandered around to the back of the inn. Outside the busy kitchen, an old man, barefooted and in tattered shirt and trousers, with matted hair and beard, was drinking a can of beer and eating a hamburger.

"Know what they give me to eat," he said when he saw the stranger. "Whatever somebody else sends back, when it's overcooked or no good. I get it," he grumbled. He peered sharply at the stranger. "You new here?" The stranger nodded. "You a friend of his—Koy's?" The stranger shook his head. "But you know who he is?" The stranger nodded. "Do something for me? He's never paid me for this place. They promised, but they never did. I keep asking Eagle and he just laughs and gives me a can of beer. Plenty of beer—no money."

"Who are you?" asked the stranger.

"Matthew Crumb. I owned this place. I mean, I still do, if they don't pay me, wouldn't you say?"

"Possession is nine tenths of the law," said the stranger.

"I was mayor of this here town. I was Governor-General. Now they make me sleep in the cellar. Give me burned hamburgers."

"Governor-General?" said the stranger.

The old man grinned slyly.

"I gave myself that title after everybody else left. But I was elected mayor, fair and square, in the old days."

"Did you see that girl in the cage?"

"I did. Looks like a sweet girl. They're a bad lot."

"What do they have in mind for her?"

Matthew Crumb shook his head.

"Do you know who she is?" Again, Crumb shook his head.

"She's the daughter of Colonel Weeks of the Jungle Patrol."

Matthew stared at the stranger. He'd always admired the Patrol. That pretty girl who called him "sir," the Colonel's daughter? Then he shook his head again.

"I don't know. I keep outa their business. They keep outa mine."

"What kind of business do you have?"

"I—" He sat quietly for a moment, staring at the half eaten sandwich. "I usta do a lot, mister. Say," he said suddenly glaring at the stranger. "Who are you, asking all this?"

"Your friend."

The old man peered at him through the darkness, his face softening.

"My friend? Do I know you?"

"Now you do. Good-bye, Matthew Crumb. I'll see you again."

Matthew Crumb stared after the tall broad-shouldered stranger as he disappeared into the darkness. He took a gulp from the can.

"My friend," he said softly, as beer dribbled down his chin. No one had spoken to him like that for years. Except that girl, the Colonel's daughter.

Coming out of his room, Eagle, the lawyer, saw a tall man walking down the corridor. There were many new men here now. Who was this one?

"Hello there," he called.

The man looked back and nodded. He was big, wearing dark wrap-around sunglasses that completely covered his eyes.

"Hi," said the stranger, and walked on.

"Just a minute," said Eagle.

But the stranger waved without stopping and went out through a door that led into the alley. Curious, Eagle followed quickly and looked into the alley, expecting to see the man. But he was gone. It was a long alley. He should still have been in sight, even in the dark. Unless he went straight up in the air. Eagle stifled an impulse to look up into the air, snorting. After all, the man didn't have wings. He went back to the casino, wondering.

The casino was going full-blast. Practically the entire population of Killer's Town was there tonight, wagering, drinking, wenching. Pilot was there with his blond and brunette. At the dice table the escaped lifers, Gusty and Greasy, and "mad dog" Pretty with his black pal Moogar, the only native hoodlum in the town. Pretty was gambling as he did everything else—recklessly. Eagle found Koy at the roulette table standing beside the croupier, Sharp, who looked like his name, clean and hard like a razor; Koy never gambled, but enjoyed watching his crooked games take the suckers.

"Killer, you see a big guy with a hat and coat and sunglasses?"

"Yeah."

"Know him?"

"No. Didn't he come on the plane with you?"

"No."

"Maybe he came on the boat with Fats. Hey, Fats."

Fats, a former pro wrestler, waddled over.

"You bring that guy here with the sunglasses?"

"I didn't bring no guy with sunglasses."

"That big guy went through here earlier. See him?"

"I seen him. A new guy with sunglasses. I figured he came in with Pilot."

"I came in with Pilot. With Pug and Ossie, the limeys." Koy looked around the room, then spoke softly.

"The guy must be a cop, maybe a spy, maybe a narc. Send Gutsy and Greasy out to find him. But keep it quiet. I don't want any panic. I don't want the games to stop. We're doing too good. If everybody starts running around, the games stop and we lose."

"What'll they do with this guy? You want him hurt?" "Enough so he'll talk. Find him, bring him to my office. Keep it quiet."

"Got you, chief."

The order was passed on to Gutsy and Greasy, the two escaped lifers from the Bangalla prison. These two ranked along with Sport and Fats as the roughest and ugliest bruisers in the town.

"Who are we looking for?" said Gusty, swinging a blackjack.

"Big guy with sunglasses."

"Yeah. Seen him earlier in the street. Boss wants him worked over?"

"Not too much. We want to ask him questions. Maybe afterward." The two men went out into the dark street .

"How'll we know him when we see him."

"Sunglasses."

"At night?"

"That's what they said."

"Must be a kook."

"Yeah. You go around that way. I'll go through the alley. Meet in back by the kitchen. If you see anything, yell." The two men separated, moving cautiously through the dark. Above in her cage, Caroline looked down, wondering about the stealthy figures, wondered if she'd ever get out of this cage and this town. She'd been in it all day. It was inhuman. Yet she dreaded the moment they'd take her out There was a sharp yell from the alley at the side. She strained her eyes, but could see nothing. What was going on in this town of terror?

As Greasy moved slowly in the dark alley, straining his eyes to see ahead, he held the blackjack in position, ready to strike at the first shadow. But a shadow struck first. A fist whipped out of the darkness, hitting him flush on the jaw. He had only an instant to react and let out a terrified yelp. Then he dropped heavily to the ground. Gutsy had just turned the other corner when he heard the sound, as if a hound dog had had someone step on his paw. Was that Greasy? Gutsy raced around to the alley clutching a lead pipe, and saw a figure on the ground. He rushed to it, bending down for a closer look. It was Greasy.

"Greasy," he started to say. But that was all as he suddenly passed into oblivion. Something hit him from the side with the force of a sledge hammer. He didn't even have time to yelp. Still wearing his hat, topcoat, and sunglasses, the Phantom bent over Gutsy, picked him up, and moved out of the alley with him over Ids shoulder. Light from the bar and casino came through the windows with music, excited laughter, and shouts. The Phantom, carrying the man over his shoulders, paused at the corner of the building. There was a heavy trellis there he'd noticed earlier. He started up the trellis with his load. In her cage, Caroline watched wide-eyed as the climbing man materialized out of the darkness. She gasped.

"Shh," he hissed as he came nearer.

In the casino, Koy sat at the bar and watched Pretty at the dice table. The crazy kid was having a run of luck, and two of the "ladies" were draped around him, helping him rake in the money. Koy scowled. If the mad dog had enough sense to quit, he'd be way ahead. But that type never quit. And when he lost, as he must, he'd start to boil and make trouble. That one was bound to make trouble sooner or later. He'd be ready for him. Eagle walked by. Koy gestured to him.

"They find that stranger yet?"

"I'll see if they're in your office. Should be by now."

Eagle left, then returned. "No sign of them."

"Send Fats and Sport out to find them," snarled Koy. Fats and Sports were in the middle of a double sirloin in the dining room and wanted to finish that first, but Eagle sent them out, angry and grumbling.

"Cook'll keep the sirloin warm. Find those guys."

They found Greasy in the alley, out cold. They looked at his face in the light coming from the casino window.

"What's that on his face?"

"I dunno. Get Eagle."

Eagle came out, had a look, then rushed back for Koy to tell him about Greasy. Moogar, the black hoodlum, was at the bar getting drinks and caught something of Eagle's report. He followed them into the alley. Koy bent over the recumbent figure.

"Is he dead?"

"No. Knocked out, like he was hit with a brick."

"What's that on his jaw? Some kinda mark. Did he have that before?"

"No. Not that. Looks like—here, light a match, have a good look."

"Jeez, looks like a skull."

"Yeah, a death's head."

Moogar, still holding the two drinks, took a quick look, then pressed back against the wail, his eyes wide.

"Listen, you know what that is?" he said.

"You keep quiet about this. Where's the other one, Gutsy? Maybe he did this."

"Why would he? They're pals."

"Anyhow, that mark----"

"Will you listen, you guys," said Moogar. "That mark -"

"Keep out of this and keep your trap shut," said Koy angrily to Moogar. He'd seen the black man with Pretty—the two were buddies. That was enough to put Moogar in Koy's bad book. Sport and Fats had circled the inn, and found nothing.

"How about the girl up there in the cage? She might have seen something."

They looked up at the cage. The shape inside was vague against the dark sky.

"Go up and get her and bring her to my office. I'll talk to her," said Koy, suddenly remembering the trim beauty of the Colonel's red-haired daughter. Fats and Sport grinned and went inside the inn.

"Eagle, get some of the other boys, Scarface and Slim, to look for that guy Gutsy. I think he's playing games."

"Yeah, but how about the guy they were supposed to find with the sunglasses?"

"Yeah, find him too," said Koy, now eager to see the young girl in his office. As he started into the inn, he heard a voice from above. Fats and Sport had gone up to the top floor and pulled the cage near the window.

"Hey, boss," said Fats.

"What?" said Koy, looking up.

"Come up here."

"What do you mean, come up there? I told you, bring her to my office."

"She's not here."

"What do you mean, she's not there?"

"Come up, see," said Fats, and there was an edge of panic in his voice. Koy raced into the inn, up the stairs. What could have happened? Was the girl dead? Had some kook gotten into the cage, assaulted, and killed her before he, Killer, could get hold of her, ruining his own plans for her?

Furious, he went up the stairs, three at a time. Moogar followed. Reaching the top-floor window, Koy peered out Fats and Sport had pulled the cage in. There was a body on the floor of the cage. Not the girl. A man.

"Who in hell is that?" said Koy.

"It's Gutsy."

"How in hell did he get in the cage?"

"I dunno. Maybe he came up after the girl."

"Then where's the girl?"

"I dunno."

"What happened to Gutsy?"

"He got slugged. Out cold, just like Greasy."

"The girl couldn't do that."

"No. Like Greasy—see his jaw?"

Sport had a flashlight. The beam was on the escaped lifer's jaw. The same mark as on Greasy. The Death's Head.

"I told you, you fools. You wouldn't listen. That's the Sign of the Skull—the Phantom! He's here!" shouted Moogar, his eyes wide with terror.

CHAPTER 10

While Koy and his men were looking at Gutsy in the cage, the Phantom and Caroline were lying flat on the sloping tile roof, only a few yards away in the darkness. They clung to the peak of the roof, side by side, and could hear the voices of the men. Caroline began to tremble. Her arms ached.

"Oh," she sighed.

"Shh," warned her unknown companion.

"I'm slipping," she whispered, feeling weak and dizzy.

The ground was four stories below. The tiles were slippery. Her fingers and hands were numb. She clung with all her strength, but felt her fingers starting to lose their grip.

"Help me," she whispered in sudden panic but before she'd finished the brief sentence, a strong arm grasped her back, holding her firmly against the roof. She sighed, feeling secure and safe. The arm was like iron. Her cheek was against the cool tile, but she could hear the men's voices, so near, getting louder, angrier.

"Who's playing games here?" said Koy. That cage was locked. I had the only key—"

Sport turned his flashlight on the lock. They stared: It was obvious what had happened. The heavy iron lock had been twisted off as though it were tin foil, as if by a giant hand. And on the lock—that mark again—the skull!

"Like I told you, it's the Phantom's mark," said Moogar.

"Will you shut up that talk about phantoms, you loony!" shouted Koy, hitting him hard with the back of his hand. Moogar fell against the window.

"Get Gutsy outa that cage. Bring him to. Find out what happened to him," said Koy.

"What about the girl?" said Fats.

"What about her, you stupid tub of lard? Find her. Find that guy with the sunglasses," shouted Koy. A few men had gathered below in the street. Word had gotten around about the cage. Pretty was down there with Frenchy and Dutch, and the rest.

"Hey, Moogar," yelled Pretty. "What's going on up there?"

Moogar leaned out of the window, nursing his jaw where Koy had hit him.

"Girl's gone. Phantom did it. Phantom's here," he shouted. "What?"

Koy slammed Moogar against the wall, his heavy hands at his throat.

"Any more of that jungle rot out of you, and you're a dead duck. You got that?"

Moogar choked and nodded. Koy banged his head against the wall, then turned away from him.

"Watch that dumb idiot," he said to Sport. "If he makes any trouble, finish him." The men left the room carrying Gutsy. Moogar looked again at the Skull Mark on the lock, then followed. No question about it. That was the mark. The Phantom was somewhere nearby.

The casino and bar were empty now. Men were milling around in the big lobby, aware that Greasy and Gutsy had been laid out by somebody. But who?

As they descended the stairs to the office, carrying the heavy Gutsy, Koy gave his orders to Eagle.

"Get all our guys out with guns to find the girl and the guy with sunglasses. How far can they get?"

"How about all the rest of the guys?"

"Keep them in the bar and casino. We don't need them, we need their dough," said Koy.

But when they reached the lobby, it was filled with men from the bar and casino. They were buzzing with the mystery of the girl and the cage.

"Hey, Koy, where's the redhead?" yelled Pretty.

"None of your business," said Koy. "Now all of you guys get back to the bar and casino and have fun. This is nothing to bother anybody."

All watched as Gutsy was carried down the stairs into Koy's office.

"Yeah? Who laid him out?" said Pretty.

"I told you, none of your business," snapped Koy.

"Maybe it is our business if somebody's taking potshots at the guys," said Finger. "We're paying for protection here."

"Right! Paying and paying!" yelled Frenchy.

"You can say that again," said Ossie.

Koy looked around. He was facing a possible riot, but his own men were in the doorways with rifles now—Fats, Sport, Banana, Scarface, Slim, and Spaghetti.

"You got protection. Any complaints?" he said, and his men raised their rifles. Frenchy, Ossie, Fingers, and the others looked at each other.

"Okay, Koy," said Fingers. "What do you want us to do?"

"Nothing. Go back to the bar and casino. Enjoy yourselves."

"Sure, lose your money to Koy's crooked table," said Pretty. Koy glared at the smiling "mad dog." He was asking for it. Then Moogar stepped up and took Pretty's arm.

"Come, kid," he said. "Like he said, have fun. While you can."

"What do you mean by that?"

"I'll tell you," said Moogar, pulling him away.

The men drifted back into the bar and casino. Koy's riflemen moved into the street, searching dark corners for the girl and the man with sunglasses.

On the roof, the Phantom had pulled the girl up so that they were now straddling the apex. There were no lights near them; they could not be seen from below.

"Who are you?" she whispered.

"A friend of your father's," he whispered back.

"Are you in the Patrol?"

"In a way."

He turned away from her as he removed his hat and sunglasses. When he turned back, she was amazed to see that his head was hooded and his eyes masked. She gasped.

"Are you a thief?"

"No. Shh." He pointed down.

Below they could see Koy's men with rifles, moving through the dimly lighted street. Now she watched as he removed his scarf and topcoat, folding them and laying them over the apex of the roof. Then he wiggled slightly, removing his trousers. She stared. In the semi-darkness, she could see a powerful form, clad in a skintight dark costume and boots. Guns on either hip were in holsters hanging from a broad gunbelt. There was an insignia on the belt, but she couldn't make it out. It was all so weird. Who was this man? Did her father have friends who wore masks? In spite of everything, she began to giggle. He quickly covered her mouth with a big hand.

"Shh," he said.

"Sorry," she whispered. "It's all so strange up here with you."

He nodded, then took her arm. They started to work their way across the roof, then suddenly stopped. He pointed down. Two of the riflemen were moving in the dark alley just below them. The masked man held her until the riflemen were gone.

"It'll be tough getting off this roof," he told her softly. They had gotten onto the roof from the top of the cage. They couldn't go back that way. Too exposed. At the side, above the alley, there was a balcony at the second-floor level. But how could they reach that from this slippery tile roof? While he considered this, a soft voice spoke behind them. The girl was amazed at the stranger's reaction. At the sound of the first soft syllable—almost before the sound, it seemed to her—the stranger had a gun in his hand, taken from the holster in a movement too fast to follow with the eye. They looked back. Just over the apex of the roof, the matted hairy head of Matthew Crumb peered at them.

"This way," he whispered.

They made their way along the apex to him. His head was sticking out of a skylight that had been covered with tiles like the roof. He disappeared from sight. The Phantom peered into the opening, lowered the girl into it, then dropped into it himself. They were in an attic room, filled with musty old trunks, broken furniture, the dust of years. The renovators had never reached this place.

"I watched," said Matthew Crumb softly. "This sweet girl, the daughter of the Colonel of the Jungle Patrol. You called me sir. I always liked the Patrol. And you, you said you were my friend." the garrulous old man stopped, seeing the strange costume for the first time.

"But I saw you climb onto the roof. Are you the same man?"

"I am your friend."

The old man nodded happily. Yes, that was the voice.

"These are evil men, and they planned to hurt this sweet child," he continued.

"We know," said the Phantom. "There's a balcony on the second floor. Can you show us the way?"

They followed him quietly through the empty corridors. There were snores from a few rooms, but they met no one. They reached a closed door. The Phantom, gun in hand, opened it slowly and peered in. It was empty.

"Thank you. We'll meet again, friend Matthew Crumb," he said.

Matthew Crumb folded his hands and looked at them wistfully, sorry to see them go. Caroline bent over and quickly kissed him.

"Thank you, sir," she said, and the door closed behind them. Matthew walked slowly down the hall. The quick touch of those soft lips. Friend. Sir. There were tears in his red-rimmed eyes.

A few men had returned to the bar. Koy peered in to see if the tables were busy. He saw the handsome Pilot at a table with three women. Koy bristled. Eagle had told all his men to get out and hunt. Pilot was with his women. He walked to the table. They were all laughing at a joke, then frozen when confronted by the grim figure.

"Didn't you get my order? I sent all my guys out to find the girl and that guy with sunglasses."

Pilot looked at him coolly, maintaining his bravado in front of his girls.

"I'm no flunky and I'm not one of your gun boys. I'm a pilot. That involves enough dirty work for you."

Koy moved in fast, and dumped the table, bottles, and glasses onto the laps of Pilot and the girls. The girls screamed and one fell over backward in her attempt to get clear of the table. Pilot jumped to his feet, his neat jacket dripping with gin.

"You thick-headed greaseball!" he shouted, moving toward Koy with clenched fists. He stumbled slightly, half drunk and reckless. Koy waited, then swung, hitting him on the side of his jaw. Pilot fell to one knee. The girls cowered in a corner, sobbing and brushing their stained dresses. Sport had entered and stood with a rifle at the ready.

"You're lucky you're my pilot, my only pilot, flyboy," said Koy. "If there was anybody else who could fly that crate, I'd rub you out like a bug."

Then he aimed a kick at Pilot's groin. Pilot turned to catch the blow on his hip, then fell over to the floor. Koy stood over him, working himself into the murderous rage that always surged up in him when someone was helpless before him.

"Now you get out and find that guy, and that girl, or we'll bury you in the cesspool and find another pilot," he shouted. Sport came alongside and took Koy's arm. He recognized the rage building up in him.

"You need him, boss. He's the only pilot we got."

Koy nodded and let himself be pulled away.

"Do like he said now," said Sport to the recumbent Pilot. Pilot staggered to his feet and swayed out of the room, avoiding the looks of the frightened girls. He staggered alone into the dark alley, then leaned against a wall. He was bitter, humiliated, sick at what had happened to him. If he had a bomb, he'd blow up the whole town.

"I'm a pilot," he said angrily to the world in general. "I'm not one of these lousy scum." And he went on in that vein, cursing Koy, all his men, and Killer's Town in general. It was at that moment, as if he hadn't had enough for one night, when something, or someone, dropped on him, taking him to the ground. Then he was flat on his back, a heavy foot on his chest. He stared at a vague figure. But he could see the glint of a gun pointed at his head.

"Not a sound. Pilot," said a deep voice.

Confused, amazed, dizzy, Pilot did as he was told. All the fight was out of him. Then he heard the voice again.

"Now, Caroline."

As he looked up, he could vaguely see a figure dropping from a second-floor balcony. A girl. The girl. With one foot still on Pilot's chest to hold him down, the stranger caught the girl in his arms. Pilot heard her exhale deeply in relief. All were motionless for a moment as the stranger looked about. Then Pilot was pulled to his feet, facing a gun. Behind the gun was a masked face, framed by a dark hood.

First Koy, now this. Too much. Pilot's legs sagged. His eyes closed. If only he could faint. He tried, but couldn't. The stranger straightened him up and shook him.

"Pull yourself together," said the deep voice. "We're going to the plane. We stop for no one. Understand?"

Pilot nodded dumbly, trying to get his bearings. Where was the man with the sunglasses? But he was given no time for questions or answers. The stranger gave him a slight shove, and started him toward the wharf, following a step behind with the girl. Pilot couldn't see or feel the gun, but he sensed it was pointing at the back of his head.

They reached the wharf without being seen. Then a man stepped out of the shadows with a rifle. It was Fats, the former wrestler.

"Hey, Pilot," he called in his raspy voice. "Who's that with you?"

"I dunno," grunted Pilot, continuing to walk.

"Hey! That's the girl! Stop right there," said Fats, raising his rifle.

Pilot jumped a foot in the air as the gun behind him exploded. The noise made his ears ring. Fats was even more startled when the bullet hit his rifle, knocking it out of his hands. He stood for a moment, staring at his hands to see if they were bleeding. They weren't hit. Another bullet whistled near his head. Fats got the message, turned, and ran. Pilot, the stranger, and the girl raced onto the wharf toward the plane. The gunfire started a clamor of voices in the background, and some of the riflemen rushed out from behind buildings into the street.

"Where are they? Who fired? Turn on the searchlights. Down at the wharf," the voices shouted. Men ran back and forth. Someone reached a switch. The wharf area was suddenly brilliantly lighted in time to see Fats diving into an open warehouse doorway. Farther away, a strange, tall figure was seen for a split second jumping into the amphibian plane. As the crowd rushed to the wharf, the motors roared, the propellers whirred, and the plane started to move away from the wharf. Koy rushed out of the inn. Others were already nearing the dock. As the plane moved within easy range, they held their fire. What to do? The plane was Roy's million-dollar beauty, his pride and joy.

"What's happened? Where are they?" shouted Koy, reaching the vanguard of men. They pointed to the moving plane.

"Who's in there?" he yelled.

The men were vague. Pilot, some guy.

"The girl?"

No one knew. Koy hesitated for precious moments. If it was only Pilot, why damage the amphibian? He could always catch up with that crazy fly boy. Then Fats came out of the warehouse.

"The girl—some guy—with Pilot—in the plane," he shouted.

"Stop them," yelled Koy.

"You mean shoot at the plane?" the men asked.

"Yes. Shoot! Shoot!"

But it was too late. The amphibian was in the air, already out of range. In a moment, it was out of sight in the darkness. Then, as if correcting an oversight, the green and red wing lights flashed on briefly. Then they were gone. Koy looked around at his riflemen, at the rest of the inhabitants of Killer's Town who had poured out of the casino and the bar, out of their rooms, at the sound of the gunfire. He was stuttering with frustration, almost apoplectic. Finally, he recognized one familiar face, one who might make sense.

"Fats, you saw them. Who were they?"

"Pilot, with the girl—and some guy."

"What guy?"

"I don't know. Not like an ordinary guy. Different."

"What do you mean different?"

"Just—different Big, weird. Shot the gun right out of my hand. Could have killed me, but didn't."

Koy grabbed Fats by the lapels of his sweater jacket "Talk sense, you idiotic walking tank. Who was it?"

A voice came out of the crowd. The words came slowly. "He told you. Different. I told you before. You wouldn't listen. That was that Phantom—the Ghost Who Walks—the Man Who Cannot Die."

All the men turned toward the speaker, Moogar. It was an awesome moment under the searchlights in the quiet jungle night. Koy stared at Moogar, then turned and walked to the end of the wharf, staring into the night, wondering confused thoughts about his lost million-dollar beauty. Pretty, standing next to Moogar, shivered.

"You're a kook, a real kook, jungle boy," he said, trying to make a joke. Nobody laughed.

CHAPTER 11

Randolph Weeks paced back and forth in his office as he had done all day. The agonizing bind he found himself in had not changed since those lights blazed in his eyes at the gates of Killer's Town. The sound of his daughters faint voice, "I'm . . . I'm all right, daddy," echoed in his head. In response to his question, "Caroline, have they hurt you?" Her frightened answer, "No, daddy." And then that arrogant mocking male voice, "No, daddy—not yet." Those words—not yet—were torturing him. All he had to do, they said, was remove the Patrol observers and they'd free her. Or had they actually said that? He couldn't remember. It didn't matter. He knew that blackmailers were never satisfied, that one surrender would be followed by a further demand. Yes, he knew all of this so well, but his lifetime of knowledge and experience wasn't helping Caroline. Not yet. His child—with those killers in a cage! So he paced and talked to himself, trying to find an answer, but there was no good answer. Then his phone rang.

It was a report from the Patrol observation post outside Killer's Town. There had been sporadic gunfire, a plane had taken off, now all was quiet. Gunfire? Caroline in the middle of a gang war? That settled it. If the Patrol or police couldn't help her, he would. Quietly, and methodically, he took an automatic rifle from the wall rack, and loaded it with ammunition from his desk. While getting extra ammo clips from his closet he noticed some grenades brought in from a raid on a railroad robber gang. Grenades. He'd blow down those gates. He stuffed the ammo clips and grenades into his bush-jacket pockets, and strode to the door. Two patrolmen waiting there grabbed him. They'd been keeping an eye on their leader.

"No, Colonel, you can't go out there."

"Let go of me. That's an order, Morgan," shouted Weeks, struggling to reach the door. The men held him.

"We're not going to let you go out and get yourself killed," shouted Sergeant Morgan as they struggled with him in the middle of the room.

"They've got my child out there, goddamn you. Let me go," shouted Weeks, managing to pull back from the two. He pointed the automatic rifle at the two panting men. "Stand aside."

Morgan, a sturdy Patrol veteran, stepped before the open door.

"No sir," he said. "You'll have to shoot me, Colonel!"

"May I come in?" said Caroline Weeks.

For a split second, the men remained frozen in place like a scene in a moving picture that suddenly stops. Then Morgan stepped aside as Caroline rushed into her father's arms. The corridor beyond the door was filled with noisy patrolmen who'd seen Caroline come in. All had been living with the anguish of the Colonel, and now they laughed and cheered.

When the noise subsided. Weeks stepped back to look at her. Beyond a slight accumulation of dust—she hadn't had a chance to wash since her jungle ride the day before—and ever so faint new worry lines near her young eyes, she looked the same as ever.

"It's a miracle," said Weeks. "How did you get here?" Caroline was still trying to catch her breath.

"Let me rest for a minute," she said.

Weeks nodded to the patrolmen. They left the room, closing the door, leaving father and daughter together. Then slowly, Caroline told him the whole story right to the dash for the plane.

"Did you know who the masked man was?" he said.

She laughed and shook her head.

"He said he was a friend of yours. I must say he was charming, though rough. But he was masked. You know, like a crook. I thought he must have been one of them, who'd fallen out with the rest and decided to get away." Weeks nodded. That would all make sense to her.

"But where is he now?"

"Oh," she said, looking perplexed, "he said he was going back there. To that awful place. If he had a fight with them, why would he go back?"

"Caroline, how did you get to my office?"

"The plane landed at the Patrol wharf. The guard there brought me here in his car."

"Did anyone back there hurt you?"

"Not really. They said some awful things. But I don't know what would have happened to me if he hadn't come," she said. And she suddenly burst into tears. He put his arm around her.

"Have a good cry. You've been a brave girl, but you've earned a good cry," he said softly.

"Excuse me. I just suddenly----" she said, still sobbing.

She took a tiny kerchief from her pocket and dabbed at her eyes.

"Daddy, who was that masked man?"

"Are you certain he was masked?"

"Oh, yes. And some kind of odd costume."

"Odd. How?"

"Unusual."

"Caroline you've seen a man I've wondered about for forty years," he said.

"Forty years? He's a young man," she said.

"How young?" he asked, suddenly inquisitive.

"I don't know. Twenty-five. Maybe thirty but no more."

"Tell me more about him."

"I've told you all I know. Who is he?"

"Caroline, for two hundred fifty years, jungle patrolmen have been asking the same question. In all that time, you're the only one who has knowingly seen him."

"Two hundred fifty years? What are you talking about, daddy?"

He led her to the wall, to the organization chart of the Jungle Patrol, and pointed to the name at the top. Commander.

"Caroline, you've been with the unknown leader—our Commander."

In the amphibian plane, Pilot glared at the Phantom. "Who in hell are you?" he asked angrily.

'That doesn't matter," said the Phantom.

Pilot was at the controls as they flew over the dark sea near the coast.

"Are you out of your mind, wanting to go back to that

place?" he said, watching closely as his masked captor put the gun back in his holster.

"What's your part in all this dirty business at Killer's Town?" said the Phantom.

"Nothing. I'm a pilot—a truck driver. I bring them in and take them out. Who they are or what they do is none of my business."

"Just an innocent chauffeur, you might say."

"Yeah. Innocent. Say, this crate is loaded with gas. We can make Naples or Lisbon. We can sell her for a quarter million, maybe a half million, easy. What do you say?"

The Phantom smiled.

"Innocent pilot? Would you risk stealing from Killer Koy?"

"He'd have to find me first," continued Pilot casually, noting they were near their destination, the wharf of Killer's Town. With his free left hand, he casually took hold of a heavy monkey wrench that was concealed next to his seat.

"Look, mister, don't you want to change your mind? Killer will finish you for sure. Probably me too for letting that girl get away."

"If you choose to work for hoods, you have to take your chances."

"I've been taking chances all my life. This is one I don't want. Have you seen Killer when he gets sore? He goes crazy, berserk. He uses a knife. What do you say, pal, do we turn around and blow?"

"We do not. Keep on course."

"You're the boss, pal," said Pilot, suddenly swinging the heavy monkey wrench at the back of the hooded head.

In Killer's Town, the sound of the approaching plane was heard. Koy rushed out of the inn with Eagle and his escort of armed men. (Koy no longer moved without Fats and Sport or other riflemen with him at all times. There was no safety in this den of thieves.) Koy stared unbelievingly into the dark. Could that be his million-dollar beauty? Impossible. Who would bring it back? Not Pilot. Then who? Maybe it was another plane, a military plane. He waited behind a corner of the warehouse with his men, just to make sure. Then it came out of the darkness, white and gleaming in the reflected wharf lights and hit the water with a big splash. It was the amphibian. Shouting, they rushed to the wharf.

A minute before, inside the plane, Pilot had swung at the hooded figure. He never quite knew what happened next. The figure moved so fast the action was blurred. Pilot's swinging arm was halted in midair by a grip of iron. The impact was as though he'd hit a stone wall. At the same moment, a fist crashed on his jaw and the scene ended in darkness for Pilot. He slumped over the controls. The Phantom quickly threw him to one side, grabbed the controls, and guided the plane safely onto the water near the wharf. Then while the plane was still moving slowly, he opened the door on the seaside and slid into the dark water.

The plane floated about fifty yards from the wharf, rocking slowly on the gentle waves that rolled into this protected harbor. Searchlights from the land shone on the white surface. The interior was unlighted, dark. Koy and his men stood on the wharf staring at it. The others—boarders, workers, waiters, cooks—watched from the background. There was silence, broken only by the sound of water lapping at the wharf posts. All seemed to be waiting for something to happen. Nothing did.

"Hello out there," shouted Koy.

The plane did not answer.

"Maybe it's empty," said Fats.

"You lunkhead. Can a plane land by itself?" said Koy.

"I dunno. Maybe it can," said Fats defensively.

"Can it. Eagle?" demanded Koy.

"Possible. Not probable," said Eagle.

"What kind of an answer is that? Can it, or can't it?" shouted Koy.

They all seemed to be playing for time, waiting for something to happen. The white plane, rocking on the water, seemed ominous, mysterious. Koy finally made the decision.

"Three of you guys—Sport, Slim, Banana—row out there. Pull it in."

The three big men, holding rifles, looked reluctantly at Koy, then climbed into the small dingy which sank almost to the gunwhales under their weight. Banana rowed, and all watched as they approached the plane.

"Can you see in there?" yelled Koy. "Stand up, you fathead."

Sport stood up with difficulty, almost capsizing the little craft as he grasped the heads of his companions to keep his balance. They squirmed as his fingers dug into their scalps. He peered at the plane quickly, then sat down.

"Too dark," he called. "What'll we do now?"

"Tie on a line, pull her in, you idiot," shouted Koy, using a corrosive blast of profanity that startled even this hardened crowd. There was a line in the dingy. They tied it to a strut on the plane and headed back to shore. The big plane dwarfed the dingy and its occupants, but it floated lightly on the water in their wake. The three men climbed onto the dock and tied the line to a post. Koy and his men formed a semi-circle facing the plane. The other inhabitants of Killer's Town watched intently. This was better than a movie.

"What are you waiting for, Koy?" shouted Pretty. "Go in and have a look." He was standing with Moogar.

Koy glared at him. That mad dog, he'll get it one of these days. Then he turned to his riflemen.

"Sport, Fats, Spaghetti, look in there."

The swarthy Spaghetti, veteran of many a street fight in his native Brooklyn, hesitated.

"Maybe they got a bomb planted, Killer. You know, you open the door, it goes up."

"You yellow dogs, what's there to be afraid of? Give me that flashlight," said Koy, pulling a gun out of his shoulder holster.

He turned on the light and stepped to the plane.

"Open that door. Spaghetti."

Spaghetti opened the plane door. Koy peered in, shining his beam.

"Pilot?" he said. "Pilot!"

He stepped in and shook the body lying over the controls. He touched the face. Still warm—not dead.

"Pull him out of there. It's Pilot, knocked cold." Fats and Sport pulled him out and stretched him out on the dock.

"Man, whoever hit him wasn't fooling," said Sport.

"How could he land that plane, out cold like that?" asked a voice.

"Anybody else in there?"

"No, empty."

There was a sharp gasp from Moogar.

"Look. On his jaw. Like Greasy and Gutsy. The Death's Head!"

There it was, the inch-high mark, blue, like a tattoo or a bruise. As skulls appear to do, the small mark seemed to grin derisively.

"We saw that plane land. There was nobody else in it."

"The Phantom was in it. He did that. I tell you, the Phantom is here!"

"Who's he talking about?" said London's Ossie to Pug.

"Phantom. Some kinda jungle hoodoo."

"A spook?"

"Like that."

The words spread through the crowd—Phantom, hoodoo, spook. All had seen or knew about the skull marks. All had seen the dark plane land. Some of the men shivered in the cool night air.

"Get him back to the inn," said Koy. "You guards," he called to men on the walls and near the warehouse, "keep your eyes open. If anybody looks suspicious or strange, shoot first, then ask questions."

Sport and Fats picked up Pilot and moved quickly to the inn. Others trotted behind them after a backward look at the empty plane.

"Moogar, is all this malarkey about a hoodoo for real?" said Pretty.

"Phantom, ghost who walks. No malarkey. He's real!" said Moogar, running off after the others.

Pretty watched them go. He sneered. All of them, yellow, afraid of everything, Koy most of all. Then he looked around the empty wharf. Deep shadows, waves lapping under the wood, the distant howl of a wolf. Realizing he was alone and unarmed, he started to walk rapidly toward the lighted inn where the last of the men were entering, then he broke into a run.

"Hey, Moogar," he called. "Wait for me."

There is an old jungle saying, told around campfires: *The Phantom's ways are so mysterious, even strong men become like children afraid of the dark.*

CHAPTER 12

The Phantom remained hidden under the wharf until the last man was gone. Then he swam underwater to the far side of the plane. He stayed there for a moment in the dark, only his eyes and nose above the surface of the water, and carefully inspected the wharf area. No one was visible. Even the guard at the nearby warehouse, shaken by the general hysteria, had left his dark post for a more brightly lighted place. Satisfied that he was not being observed, the Phantom quietly climbed into the amphibian. He crouched on the floor near the controls, keeping his head below the level of the glass windows. Then he switched on the radio transmitter and made a hurried call.

"Calling JP 12C. Calling JP 12C," he repeated several times. At Jungle Patrol headquarters, the patrolman operator had stepped out of the radio room to get a drink of water at the cooler in the hall. At this time of night, the air waves were usually silent.

The Phantom persisted, almost angrily. Where was the man? He didn't have much time; he couldn't remain too long in the plane and risk being seen.

"Calling JP 12C. Come in JP 12C," he repeated intensely. In the hall, the operator was lazily drinking from a paper cup, when he heard the buzzing from the radio room. Probably a routine call from one of the far-ranging Patrol cars. When on a mission, they reported periodically. No rush. They could wait. He finished his drink leisurely, stared at his reflection appreciatively in a hall mirror. "You really are good-looking, like that girl said the other night," he said aloud. Then he strolled back to the radio room. The receiver panel was buzzing.

"Hold your horses," he said as he lazily took his seat, put on his earphones, and turned up the receiver.

"Calling JP 12C," were the words he heard. "Where are you JP 12C?"

"JP 12C. Here I am. What's your hurry?" said the operator.

In the plane, the Phantom sighed with relief. If he'd been a man who used profanity, he would have used it then. But he didn't.

"This is the Commander."

The radio operator jolted with surprise, stiffened in his chair, his eyes popped, and he gasped. The unknown Commander and he had said, "What's your hurry?"

"Sir, excuse me. I didn't know who-----" he began.

The deep voice interrupted.

"Quiet. Listen. I can only say this once. Are you receiving me? Over."

"Yes sir. Over."

"Message to Colonel Weeks. Exactly as I give it to you. Bring Patrol and police at once to Killer's Town. Surround the place. Be ready to pick up the mob. Wait for my signal. Commander. Repeat. Over."

"Bring the patrol and police at once to Killer's Town. Surround the place. Be ready to pick up mob. Wait for my signal. Commander," said the operator in a quavering voice.

"Good. Out," replied the deep voice. There was a click, and the transmission had stopped. The patrolman stared at the message. The pencil was trembling in his hand. Wow! he thought, then reached for the phone that was a direct line to the Colonel's bedroom. No answer. He tried the private office. A patrolman on duty there said the Colonel was on his way home with his daughter. The operator began to ring the Colonel's home again, impatiently, then suddenly remembered Weeks had a radio-telephone in his car. He reached him as the Colonel was entering his own driveway. He delivered the message, and had to repeat it for the amazed Weeks. The Colonel uttered a happy (and unprintable) expletive, apologized to Caroline at his side, then barked back an order.

"Alert Sergeants Hill and Morgan. I want a task force of fifteen men, fully armed, ready to leave in thirty minutes. Now, get me Chief Togando at once."

He awoke Togando out of a deep sleep with the news, and quickly arranged with the startled Chief to have a police detachment join the task force.

"But what happened?" asked Togando. Like all others outside the Patrol, he had no knowledge of the existence of an unknown Commander. Weeks didn't explain, merely telling him there was a possible breakthrough at Killer's Town, that they must move now—and fast.

The Phantom slipped back into the dark water leaving scarcely a ripple, swam underwater back to the wharf, and climbed out. In the background, lights blazed from every window of the big inn. All the other restored buildings on the three blocks of the main street, containing the casino, a bar, barbershop, a small movie house (featuring hardcore pornography), and a little dance hall with a tireless brass- unged piano player, were brightly lit. Strong men like children afraid of the dark. The area at the wharf and warehouse remained dark, only because no one had remained to turn on the lights there. Grateful for the darkness, the Phantom slipped into the warehouse. Using a tiny but powerful flashlight that he carried in his belt, he prowled through the huge dark rooms filled with century-old musty dampness. The place was piled high with recently arrived supplies of all sorts, including a variety of ammunition, weapons, and explosives—enough to supply a small army. In his search, he was pleased to find a power megaphone. He carried it along for future use.

Then he worked quietly over a pile of boxes containing explosives: dynamite, shells, grenades, fuses, detonators. He carefully wired a detonator into the mass of explosives, then recovered the crates, concealing the detonator and leaving no evidence of his work. He took a small watch from a pouch on his belt. The specially made mechanism was impervious to heat, water, or pressure; it also contained a tiny radio transmitter, a submicro solid-state marvel with a range of a half mile. It now showed eleven o'clock on the pale illuminated dial. He'd made his radio call at ten-thirty. The Patrol should be on the move by now. They'd need an hour and a half to reach this place and take positions. That would give him time to do what needed to be done.

The main bar next to the inn was doing overflow business. Bottles were pouring, cash registers chiming, glasses clinking. A dozen men were crowded around a table where Koy sat with Moogar, Eagle, and some of his inner group. Sport, Fats, and Spaghetti. The attention was on Moogar, the lone black in the crowd.

"Tell us about this guy who took off with Pilot," said Koy, chewing his inevitable cigar. He chewed more than he smoked, and he had the habit of spitting out chewed tobacco straight ahead regardless of who or what was there. Everyone got into the habit of staying to one side to avoid the deluge. "Like I said, he is the Phantom," said Moogar.

The men looked at each other. What was this jungle boy talking about?

"We got to know who we're fighting," said Koy patiently. He was only patient when he was dealing with something he didn't understand, or was frightened of. "Tell us about him."

"All in the jungle know. He is the Phantom, the Ghost Who Walks—the Man Who Cannot Die," said Moogar defiantly, looking at the hard cynical faces around him.

"You mean, he's some kind of spook?" asked Sport sarcastically. Pretty was standing behind Moogar's chair. Though he shared the general disbelief, it annoyed him to see his new pal baited.

"You asked him. Let him tell you," Pretty snarled.

Koy looked at him stolidly for a moment. This mad dog would have to be taken care of soon. He turned to Eagle.

"What about Pilot? Has he come to, yet?"

"No, still out. Whoever hit him really let him have it."

"Like Ossie and Pug. Both those guys out cold. Still not talking," said Fats.

"Okay, Moogar," said Koy. "This spook, or whatever he is, what about him?"

"I told you," said Moogar. "He is the ruler of the Deep Woods—he has the strength of ten tigers—he has the wisdom of ages—he is many centuries old—he is the Man Who Cannot Die."

Koy slammed the table with his big fist.

"What is all this ignorant jungle jabber?" he shouted, losing patience and exploding a foul string of four-letter words. "Whoever hit Ossie and Pug and Pilot was no ghost, no spook!"

"You saw the Skull Marks yourself. Skull Mark on Ossie. Skull mark on Pug. Skull Mark on Pilot," shouted Moogar in return. "All the jungle knows, that is the mark of the Phantom. He is here—somewhere here!"

At that moment, all lights in the place went out. The big room was in darkness. The suddenness, the completeness of it, caused a stunned silence for moments. Then someone yelled, "Hey, the lights." Others took it up. Hearing their own voice made them feel better.

"What happened to the lights? Where's the fuse box? Somebody get the lights." Men began to move and a few started to reach for matches when a big voice boomed out of the blackness.

"QUIET!"

There was a hush. Everyone froze in place.

"KILLER, A GUN IS AIMED AT YOUR FOREHEAD, ONE INCH ABOVE YOUR EYES. IF ANYONE MOVES, THE GUN GOES OFF."

Killer's voice was heard in the dark, shrill, half-choked. "Don't nobody—don't anybody move," he said.

"Who are you?" said a tough Brooklyn voice (Pretty).

"Phantom. Ghost Who Walks," said another voice (Moogar).

"He's near the window," said another softly (Eagle).

As if in answer, the voice boomed out again, but from another direction.

"THIS TOWN IS AN ABOMINATION. IT WILL BE DESTROYED. ALL OF YOU HERE NOW MUST LEAVE, OR BE DESTROYED WITH IT."

The crowd listened in the dark. The dark was scary, so was the voice coming out of nowhere. But it was a man's voice.

"Who are you?" said Koy faintly.

"MOOGAR TOLD YOU." The voice came from still another direction.

The men listened carefully. The man behind the voice was moving from place to place. But they could hear no footsteps. "The Phantom moves on cats' feet" was an old jungle saying.

"KILLER, YOU AND YOUR MEN ARE FINISHED. YOU WILL SURRENDER TO THE JUNGLE PATROL FOR THE ABDUCTION OF CAROLINE WEEKS."

There were startled exclamations from the men near Koy.

"Shh," said Koy, moving slowly to his knees on the floor.

"THE REST OF YOU WILL BE DEPORTED TO YOUR OWN COUNTRIES, TO FACE THE JUSTICE YOU RAN AWAY FROM."

There was a low angry murmur from the men.

"Don't move, anybody," shouted Koy, a gun in one hand, his other hand over his forehead as he slowly backed under the table. "What. . . what if nobody wants to go?" he said.

"IF YOU REFUSE TO LEAVE, TAKE YOUR CHANCES ON SURVIVAL. THIS TOWN IS DOOMED. YOU HAVE ONE HOUR TO GET OUT. ALL OF YOU. ONE HOUR."

"Wait! We need time to think," said Koy, peering out from under his table. All waited in silence. But there was no answer. At the side, a door squeaked open, then closed.

"There he goes. Get him!" shouted Koy. "He's gone. Lights!"

A few matches were struck, a kerosene lamp lighted.

"Where is he? Where? Where?"

"There's Koy," said Pretty, holding up the kerosene lamp, as Koy crawled under the table. It was funny, but no one laughed.

"Killer," shouted Moogar. "Look! On your glass!"

The kerosene lamp was held close to the table. There was a Skull Mark on the glass at Koy's place at the table. All stared at it.

"He was right here!" said Moogar, his eyes wide in the pale lamplight.

A voice called from the hall—Spaghetti's.

"We found it. Killer. Somebody cut the cable."

And the lights were suddenly on. The men and women looked at each other. All were touched by strain as though they'd been through a bad storm. Spaghetti ran into the room. He was sweating and pale like the others.

"The lights went out because the cable was cut. And know what we found on the wall where it was cut?" he said.

"Like this?" said Moogar, holding up the glass with the Skull Mark on it. Spaghetti stared at it and nodded. Koy waved his gun angrily, his confidence returning.

"A ghost can't cut wires. Spread out everybody. We'll catch this joker. Nobody's making a fool out of Killer Koy."

"Killer, look on your gun," said Moogar, standing at his side.

Killer looked at his gun and almost swallowed his cigar. The Skull Mark was on the barrel of his shining automatic. He rubbed at it weakly and for a moment was speechless. He remembered as he crouched under the table, the gun held out, something had brushed by, something as light as a butterfly. Was that it? Had it been that close? Close enough to kill him in the dark? He rubbed at the mark on the gun. Whatever it was, it wouldn't rub off.

"Killer, he said we have one hour to get out of town. We better get out," said Moogar.

"Yeah," agreed a few of the watching men.

Koy breathed deeply. He'd been through too much in his tough life to let this get him.

"You guys crazy? Afraid of a spook? Look, a spook can't knock guys cold, cut wires, make marks on glasses and wood."

"How do you know?" said Moogar quietly.

"You started all this spook stuff with your idiotic jungle tripe," said Koy, trying to work up a rage. "No more of it, hear me, or as you stand there. I'll shoot you deader than a cold herring. Got it?"

Moogar nodded, clenched his, fists, but did not answer. In the background, Pretty watched, his eyes blazing.

"Now, I want all you guys to spread out, to search this town from top to bottom," he said to the crowded room. "You guys got no choice. You've got no place to go."

"You talk big with that gun in your hand," said Pretty. "If we look for this spook, you going to give us back our guns?"

Koy started to react angrily, to say no, but the crowd was with Pretty.

"Guns," said a half dozen at once. The others grunted their agreement. Someone shouted from outside the door. Fats.

"Hey, Killer," he yelled. "Come out here and look at this."

On the wall, just outside the swinging bar room doors, was a big skull mark and above it in big crude letters— ONE HOUR. All in dripping, wet black paint. Killer chewed savagely on his cigar, then spit out a wad. Fats ducked just in time.

"That joker's not going to bluff us. Know what? I figure it's one of the guys in this place, somebody trying to take over."

"Ghost Who Walks," said Moogar solemnly.

"Whoever, whatever. Move. Find him!" shouted Koy.

"Guns first," said Pretty, and a dozen others grunted in agreement.

"Okay, you guys. Fats, take them to the cellar. Give them guns, bullets. No more excuses. Find this joker," he yelled, spitting a wad of tobacco at the Skull Mark. As the men started after Fats, one of them remained standing at the wall, arms folded, a stubborn look on his face—Dutch, one of the bank robbers. His partner, Frenchy, stood near him.

"You, too," said Koy.

Dutch shook his head.

"This is none of my business. We're paying you plenty for protection. Five C's a night, half our loot. So protect us."

"Right," said Frenchy.

Koy's pent-up rage and fear exploded. His face turned red. Dutch should have recognized the danger signs, but didn't.

"I'm staying right here," he said coolly.

"You're right you are, you------!" shouted Koy, shooting point blank at him. Dutch's mouth fell open in surprise, he turned toward Frenchy, then fell to the ground. The other men, starting after Fats, stopped and turned.

"Any more?" shouted Koy, glaring at Frenchy. Frenchy looked at Dutch, lying on the ground. Then at the gun in Koy's hand. He shook his head.

"Move," said Koy. The men walked off, following Fats. Frenchy stepped over the body of Dutch and went after them without a backward glance.

As the men followed Fats through the alley to the cellar door leading to Roy's gun room, they stopped. A man was lying on the ground. Banana, the tough little hood from Chicago. Knocked cold. A Skull Mark on his jaw. All made a dash for the cellar where Fats rapidly passed out weapons.

"Not that one," said Pretty, tossing back a rusty six shooter.

"That's mine," he said, reaching for a shiny forty-five automatic. Others were similarly busy, finding their own guns, stocking up on ammunition.

"All okay?" said Fats at last.

They looked at each other, crowded in the damp cellar.

"Where's Frenchy?" someone asked.

"He was right behind me," said Sharp.

Sharp peered out the cellar, then swore. Just outside the door, in the alley, Frenchy was lying on the ground, unconscious, a Skull Mark plainly visible on his jaw. And printed on the wall, next to the cellar door THIRTY MINUTES— with the big Skull Mark in dripping black paint

"That just happened. While we were here getting our guns," said Moogar.

Fats rushed to tell Koy, as the men spread out, searching for the unknown.

"Banana and Frenchy—in the alley—-another sign on the wall, while I was handing out guns," said Fats haltingly, his big face red and perspiring. Koy nodded and then pointed to another fresh wet sign, just discovered on the sign of the Killer Hilton—THIRTY MINUTES—with the Skull Mark. Wet black paint.

Outside, all the town lights and searchlights were on now as the men, three dozen in all, moved slowly among the buildings, avoiding those places where the lights did not reach, where there were darkness and shadows. Koy stood on the veranda of the inn, a gun in each hand, staring at his hotel sign. The tension was getting to him. It came to a head when a scraggly old man lurched up to him. Matthew Crumb.

Outside Killer's Town, a line of vehicles was parked at a safe distance. Patrol cars, police cars. Police and patrolmen were assigned places at various points near the wall. All were heavily armed. Handguns, automatic rifles, riot guns. The teams moved off quietly in the darkness. Each unit carried a walkie-talkie radio. Colonel Weeks and Chief Togando established their command post in the Colonel's car near the big main gates. From there, they could keep in contact with all the teams. All the men, Patrol and police, had been briefed before leaving Mawitaan. "We wait for the signal. We don't enter the place. We wait for them to come out to us," he told them.

"Who's giving us the signal?" asked one of the senior police officers.

"X will give you the order," said Weeks, not answering specifically.

Now Weeks and Togandc waited. Each was armed. With them, a patrolman and policemen.

"We wait here?" asked Togando. "What makes you think anyone will come out?"

"Just a hunch," said Weeks, not knowing what else to say.

They were suddenly tense as a figure passed inside the gates—paused, then vanished.

"Did he see us?" said Togando.

Their car was behind a clump of bushes, their lights out

"Not likely," said Colonel Weeks. He was wrong. Matthew Crumb had seen them.

Now, as Koy stood on his veranda, fighting the fear of the unknown that was gradually seizing him, Matthew Crumb approached him.

"Mr. Koy," he said. "I been trying to have a talk with you for some time. About my money."

"Who is this?" growled Koy.

"That old bum, the one that owned this place," said Eagle.

Koy, now close to paranoia, grabbed the old man by his ragged shirt collar.

"Is this the guy who's playing those tricks, trying to scare us out, planting those marks?" he shouted.

Crumb choked and sputtered, held in Roy's tight grip.

"Cut it out," raid Eagle with a half laugh. "That old guy knock out Gutsy and Greasy and all the rest? He couldn't knock out a fly."

"Yeah," said Koy. He shoved the old man so he fell on the veranda floor, then kicked him.

"Get lost," he said.

"I'm going to the police, to the Jungle Patrol," muttered Crumb. "I'll put the law on you. I know where they are." The word "law" clanged in Koy's head. He pointed his gun at the recumbent Matthew Crumb.

"I'll blow him apart, the filthy old tramp!" he shouted. Eagle grabbed his arm.

"Come on, Killer," he said. "Let the old man be."

"Eagle," said Koy, "where's Pilot?"

"In your office."

"Let's get him. We're getting out of here."

"Getting out?" said Eagle as he ran after his boss. Koy explained as they reached his office door.

"We'll fly away for a few hours, until they find the spook. Then we come back. By that time, they'll know they got no other place to go."

"That's not a good idea," said Eagle, the lawyer, slowly, afraid to cross his only client.

"We're going," said Koy.

Pilot was sitting on the edge of the couch in the office, his head in his hands. Koy grabbed him by the hair, jerked his head up. There was a distinct Skull Mark on Pilot's jaw. His eyes were still glassy. He groaned and tried weakly to pull away. Koy held him by the hair.

"On your feet, flyboy. We're taking a trip."

Eagle helped him lift up the dazed Pilot.

"Killer, he can't fly like this. He can hardly walk."

"He'll be okay with a little air. Give him a swig of this." He took a bottle of whiskey from his desk, uncorked it, forced the opening into Pilot's mouth, and poured whiskey into him. Pilot sputtered and choked. Whiskey dribbled down his chin.

"That'll do it," said Koy. "Let's go."

"Wait, Killer. What about all that?" said Eagle, pointing to the safe.

The huge safe, as high as a man, weighing four tons, contained all the loot that had been brought to Killer's Town from the four corners of the earth. Koy's share of the heists, and all the cash, gems, and gold held in safekeeping for the others. A fortune no one, including Koy, knew exactly how much. Koy hesitated. But he was shaking with anxiety, anxious to get away.

"The stuff'll keep. No one's going to get in there. We'll be back in a couple hours. It's safer here. Besides how can we carry it? Let's go."

Walking on either side of the staggering Pilot to support him, they left the inn, and made for the wharf where the plane remained tied up. Other, men in the background, hunting the unknown, paid no attention to them. But Moogar moved near them. He understood the situation in a glance.

"Hey, Killer. Are you cutting out on us?" he called.

"Get lost," said Koy.

Undaunted, rifle in hand. Moogar strode up to him.

"You ditch us, the boys won't like that, boss or no boss," said Moogar.

"Yeah. Ask them what they think," said Koy, glancing to the side. Moogar looked inquiringly to the side, where Koy had looked. There was no one there. In that moment, Koy swung the butt end of his heavy automatic, hitting Moogar on the side of his head. Moogar dropped without a sound.

"Since when do I ask the boys what they like?" said Koy, looking at the recumbent Moogar.

"Come on, Koy, if we're going, let's go," said Eagle, holding Pilot up. Pilot was starting to move under his own power. Koy grabbed his arm and they moved to the dock.

"Where we going?" he muttered.

"For a ride, flyboy," said Koy.

Lying on the dark roof of the warehouse, the Phantom saw the scene with Moogar, then watched as the three men moved to the plane. Koy, obviously, was making a getaway. Did he know the place was surrounded? Not likely. But he was headed for the plane. On the wharf, Pilot became stubborn.

"I'm not going anywhere," he said thickly.

Koy put the big gun under his nose.

"You're flying us, boy," he said.

"Koy, I can't fly. I'm dizzy. Can't see straight," said Pilot.

"You'll be okay. Just a short trip. Let's move," said Koy.

On the roof, the Phantom aimed his own gun. It's a pity, he thought, but it has to be done. He fired toward the wharf, not at the three men, but at the gas tanks of the amphibian plane. High-octane gas is extremely combustible. Killer Roy's million-dollar beauty blew sky high with a tremendous blast, as though hit by a bomb. The three men on the wharf fell to the ground, knocked down by the explosion. Everyone in Killer's Town rushed out into the street as red and yellow flames and black smoke mushroomed into the sky like a miniature atom-bomb explosion. Outside the wall, concealed in the woods, the patrolmen and police jumped to the alert.

"What's going on in there?" asked Chief Togando.

"Wish I knew," said Colonel Weeks. And to himself, he thought, is that the signal?

But it wasn't. The big gates remained closed, locked on the inside by a heavy chain and padlock.

On the wharf, Killer sat on the rough wood staring at the blaze. Tears flowed down his cheeks.

"My beauty, my million-dollar beauty," he sobbed.

Behind him, men were yelling.

"The shot came from up there," Pretty shouted, pointing to the warehouse roof. A dozen men fired their rifles at the roof. Then all was quiet. There was a ladder leaning against the warehouse wall With a rifle in one hand and his handgun tucked in his belt, Pretty climbed up to the roof. He paused. There, painted crudely on the sheet metal, was the Skull Mark, this time in dripping red paint, with lettering above it

"Hey, guys," he called down. "Here's that skull thing again.

Know what it says now? Fifteen minutes left."

Pretty looked around the dark roof, fired a few bullets into shadowy corners, then returned to the ground.

Most of the men in Killer's Town were clustered within fifty yards of the inn, watching Pretty climb down the ladder.

Koy had gotten to his feet and, with a last look back at the burning wreck, he walked away with Eagle.

"Plane's gone. Now what?" said Eagle.

"No way out. Got to find that spook," said Koy.

At the foot of the ladder, Pretty turned to see Moogar staggering toward him.

"What happened? Spook get you, pal?" said Pretty.

Moogar reached Pretty, and sagged, holding onto his shoulder. His head was bleeding.

"Spook—huh—Koy—was trying to make a getaway, in the plane—hit me," said Moogar. He sat down heavily on a box and pressed a handkerchief against his head. The men watched as Pretty confronted Koy and Eagle.

"You tried to cut out on us, Koy," said Pretty

"So what? This is my town. I do what I want," said Koy.

"He tried to ditch us. How about that?" said Pretty, turning to the watching men. They replied with an angry muttering.

"This is my town. If you don't like it, get out. Right now. All of you," Koy shouted, directing the you to Pretty who faced him.

"Not likely," said Pretty. "We paid a month's rent. Remember?"

"Why you little-----!" Koy yelled, doubling up his fist, but Pretty swung first, hitting Koy hard on the jaw. Koy fell to the cobblestones.

"I'm taking over, you------!" said Pretty, kicking Koy in the side.

He looked around challengingly, gun in hand. The men looked at him, then at each other. Koy's men were there, the insiders like Fats and Sport, as well as the outsiders, the "guests," like Fingers and Pretty. All were armed. All slowly backed away, weapons held alertly, ready to shoot. Eagle and Sport helped Koy to his feet, half-dragging him No shots were fired until all had found cover. No one knew what would happen next. Pretty decided that. He fired a shot at Koy and Eagle who were crouched behind a corner of the warehouse. Koy returned the shot. Then all. began to fire. It was a free-for-all with bullets going in all directions, Koy's insiders versus the outsiders.

Outside the walls, the Patrol and the police heard the firing. Once more they asked each other, "What's going on in there?" And once more, Colonel Weeks thought, is that the signal? But the big gates remained closed. Now, there was a lull in the pitched battle, as men looked for a target or reloaded.

"FIVE MINUTES LEFT. GO NOW!"

The big voice had come from somewhere out of the dark sky. No one was sure just where. The men stared at each other, their mutual hatred forgotten for the moment in the face of the common, unknown enemy.

"This is too much, everything's out of hand," groaned Koy, nursing his aching jaw.

"You've got a civil war on your hands. Got to stop this first," said Eagle, the lawyer. He waved a white handkerchief in the general direction of the concealed Pretty.

"Boys—Pretty, Moogar, all of you—we got to find the spook."

"There's no spook. It's a trick of Killer's, trying to get rid of us," Pretty shouted. He fired in Eagle's direction, and the barrage began again.

The Phantom moved quietly toward the gate. There were no guards there now. The entire town was down at the wharf in the gun battle. At the gate, he peered carefully outside. He knew there was a concealed car in the bushes. It was too dark for him to be seen clearly. He moved quickly, grasped the heavy chain and big padlock, and with a single powerful twist, snapped the chain in two, then vanished in the dark. Weeks and Togando looked up quickly. "What was that?"

But once more, the steady gunfire inside the town claimed their attention. What was going on?

Once more there was a lull, as the men reloaded, or wondered what they were doing. It all seemed aimless and pointless since that spook was still in their midst. At that moment, the spook chose to speak again. The great voice boomed out

"THE GATES ARE OPEN. ONE MINUTE LEFT."

"Koy," yelled Pretty, "go to the gate!"

"No tricks?"

"No tricks."

Warily, respecting the armed truce, the men moved to the gate.

Koy, Pretty, Eagle, and a few others examined the chain. "Chain's torn apart," said Eagle.

"That chain could hold an elephant. Who could tear it?" said Koy.

"Phantom could. Phantom did," said Moogar, pressing the handkerchief against his head. "Look at the lock."

They saw it on the lock. The Skull Mark—the same mark had been floating through their heads all night.

"I've got this spook thing figured," announced Pretty to the others. "Koy hears Moogar spouting this jungle malarkey. He knows a good thing when he hears it. He's got his boys making that Skull Mark and painting that stuff, trying to scare us."

"And why would he do that?" said Eagle as Koy snorted. "Why? Keep our money, and scare us out of this town to make room for other chumps and their money," announced Pretty without hesitation. It all made sense to him.

"That's the kinda crazy idea you would come up with," snarled Koy. "Think I'd blow up my own plane, my million-dollar beauty?"

"Why not? You've got plenty of dough. Our dough. Enough to buy a dozen."

Koy turned imploringly to the crowd which was listening skeptically to Pretty. He didn't make much sense to them either. "Listen, you guys, I know nothing about the spook, but I've had just about enough of this –"

And now for the last time, the great voice boomed out of the dark sky. All froze at the familiar sound.

"THE TIME IS UP. GO."

Something in this simple announcement carried final truth. They believed it. The time was up. Go. Go where? The men began to mill around uncertainly. Some turned back toward the wharf. A few started through the gate. Pretty held them at gunpoint.

"Wait. Don't fall for his bluff. He wants to get rid of us and keep our dough."

"This is no bluff," shouted Koy. "You want this town? Take it. I'm going," he yelled as he threw open the gates.

"No, you don't, you-----!" said Pretty, and shot him in the back. Clutching the bars of the gate, Killer Koy looked at him bewilderedly as Pretty stood there grinning with his smoking gun. Mad dog—have to take care of him, thought Koy as he dropped to the ground. He vaguely heard the explosion as he blacked out.

CHAPTER 13

The explosion was enormous, not one but a series, building to a vast crescendo as the explosives in the warehouse blew up. The destruction of the amphibian plane was like a firecracker next to this. Flames and smoke soared a thousand feet. Wood and metal filled the air, crashing for a half mile around. Everyone in that area took cover as best they could. Most escaped injury. Others were less lucky. Hearing the explosion. Weeks hesitated only for a moment. This had to be the signal. Then a slight beep on his walkie-talkie told him. The deep voice he knew so well, coming from somewhere: "This is it, Colonel Weeks. Take over."

That was all, but it was enough. He just had time to alert his teams, when the gates were flung open and armed men rushed out of Killer's Town.

Searchlights hit them in the face, and voices shouted at them through megaphones.

"We are the Jungle Patrol and the police. Surrender. You are under arrest."

The men were caught by surprise.

They leaped into the bushes, some behind trees, some running back into the town, taking cover as best they could, and opened fire on the teams. The teams replied with a concerted blast. It was the closest thing to modern warfare the jungle had ever seen. Several criminals tried to escape over the walls. They threw blankets over the broken glass on the wall and started over, when powerful searchlight beams sprang out of the dark to pin them there. Automatic rifles were trained on them; they had nowhere to go but into the waiting Patrol cars. The battle between the criminals of Killer's Town and the law was short. The relentless pressure of the mysterious Phantom, the civil war waged among themselves, the earth-shaking explosions, and now the trap formed by the Patrol and the police sapped whatever fight remained in them. None carried enough ammunition for a sustained effort. So after the first minutes of gunfire, they dropped their empty guns and began to surrender.

At the first sound of the Patrol guns, Pretty and Moogar had raced back into the town. They ran to the small gate near the wharf area. The wharf itself was blazing, and small shells and grenades were still detonating inside the inferno that had been the warehouse. Reaching the gates, they looked back to see that no one had followed or noticed them in the confusion. But one had noticed them. As they started for the gate, a scraggly old man blocked the way. Matthew Crumb. He held a rusty old saber in his hands, found in one of his ancient attics. The old man waved the saber threateningly.

"I saw you shoot Mr. Koy," he shouted. "He owed me money for this town and never paid."

Pretty raised his gun to shoot the old man, but Moogar touched his arm. He knew Matthew Crumb and pitied the old derelict.

"Mr. Crumb," he said, "you can have your town back. Nobody wants it any more."

"There's been crime in this town and killing but the time's come for justice," said Matthew Crumb defiantly. "And you're not getting away," he said, pointing the saber at Pretty, "because I seen you shoot Mr. Koy and I'm handing you over to the Jungle Patrol."

"Wait, let me talk to him," said Moogar as he saw the wild light in Pretty's eyes. But Pretty grinned and fired.

Matthew Crumb dropped the saber, clutched his stomach, and dropped to the ground.

"You didn't have to do that," shouted Moogar.

"You coming with me or you going to stand here and argue?" said Pretty, the wild light still in his eyes.

"Let's go."

They jumped over Matthew Crumb and ran to the water. In the distance they saw a Jungle Patrol speedboat in the flickering firelight of the burning wharf. A searchlight beam sprang out toward them like a long finger and a voice boomed through a megaphone.

"Stay where you are. You're under arrest."

Pretty and Moogar dashed behind a clump of trees near the

shore.

"Are you kidding?" yelled Pretty.

He fired a quick shot at the distant boat. Then the two men raced into the bushes as a barrage of bullets zinged into the trees behind them. Ahead was the swamp fringing the shore. They plunged into it, and began to move as fast as they could away from the sea. They could hear the roar of the motorboat following them along the coast. A voice called through the megaphone; an occasional bullet whizzed near them. Soon, motorboat and voice became faint, then were gone as they went deeper into the swamp.

They had reached a small area of dry ground when Pretty stopped suddenly. His mouth fell open, his body tensed as he drove his fist angrily into the palm of his other hand, then dug his fingers into his hair.

"What's the matter?" said Moogar, amazed by this sudden anger that seemed to come for no reason.

"Matter?" screamed Pretty between clenched teeth. "We got to go back."

"Back there? You crazy?"

"The diamonds. All the stuff we brought from New York. In Koy's safe. That's the matter," shouted Pretty, shaking with fury. He turned and started to go back. "Come on," he growled.

Moogar shook his head and didn't move. His rifle was in his hands.

"We can't go back. Don't be crazy. Cops and Patrol took over the place. They're cruisin', looking for you and me right now. Know what they'd do if they found us, Pretty?"

Pretty stared at him, too frustrated to talk.

"In this country, they hang you, man. They hang you by the neck till you're dead. I'm not going back."

Pretty breathed deeply, then sat on the ground. His moods could change like the breeze.

"After all that in New York. And that's not all. All that other stuff sitting in that safe. The cash from the bank job. You know, Frenchy and Dutch, and that stuff Sharp brought from Hong Kong—jewels and drugs. And the London heist, Ossie and Pug. And lots more we never knew about. We coulda blown that damn safe, brought it with us. What a fool. I was stupid. Stupid," he shouted, his voice rising. He pounded his legs, lowered his head, and, to Moogar's amazement, began to cry.

While the battle went on at the gates and wall, the Phantom roamed through the alleys and buildings of the town. A few thugs had hidden in cellars and attics. He flushed some of them out with gas grenades he'd brought from the warehouse. They came out, staggering, choking and blinded by the fumes to perceive the grim, menacing figure, masked and hooded like a medieval executioner. The sight was enough to send most of them stumbling in a panic to the gates and into the hands of the waiting Jungle Patrol. For the remainder, a few well-placed shots within an inch of a nose or big toe sent them hurriedly after the others.

The Phantom found Matthew Crumb lying at the small gate near the wharf. He knelt beside him and held the frail old man in his arms.

"Who shot you, Matthew?"

The old man coughed and choked.

"That one they call Pretty," he gasped, talking with difficulty. "He was the worst. Shot Mr. Koy in the back. Good riddance. He was a rat. Never did get my money." He had a fit of coughing, then went on, "I'm gonna kick that whole crowd out. Bunch of bums. Say," he said in sudden alarm, "did that poor girl get out?"

"She did, Matthew, thanks to your help. Where did Pretty go?"

"That way," he said, pointing feebly. "Had the black with him."

Matthew relaxed. He smiled and looked at the masked face.

"I know who you are," he said. "I saw the mark. I mean . . . are you really him . . . the one?"

"Yes, Matthew," said the Phantom, as he felt the old man's life slipping away.

"Heard about you for years. Always wanted to see you. Here you are. Now ain't that something."

He looked toward the smoldering warehouse.

"Who done that?"

"I did. Sorry, but I had to to get them out."

"I know. Like we usta, to clear cobra out of the sugar cane," he said, his mind wandering to other times and places. "You did good." Those were his last words. His eyes remained open, staring as the light and shadow of the flames flickered across his face. The Phantom closed his eyes, then walked across the town carrying Matthew Crumb in his arms. He went to the veranda of the inn, the former Governor's mansion. There was new furniture. He put Matthew on the chaise longue, and folded his arms on his chest. Matthew was back where he belonged, on his own front porch.

The Phantom went through the inn, searching every room from roof to cellar. The huge mansion was empty. He paused in one large, luxuriously furnished room that held a huge safe. Koy's office. He looked at it thoughtfully. The loot of Killer's Town must be kept somewhere. Probably here. He examined the safe. It was big, heavy, old-fashioned. He looked at the big dial, and, half-smiling, twirled it. Then, kneeling by it, he began to twirl and listen. He had once captured a celebrated safecracker who had hidden in the jungle. In the long trip back, the wily criminal talked about the tricks of his calling. From time to time after that, it had amused the Phantom to practice what he had been told. He had found a warehouse full of new and old safes, all empty and open. He closed one, spun the combination dial, then tried to reopen it. That took three hours. The next one took an hour. He opened a dozen more in the next hour. In his pursuit of evildoers, this ability had become useful on more than one occasion. This was such an occasion. He opened Koy's safe in five minutes, and quickly examined the contents: loot worth several millions. He closed the safe door, leaving it unlocked, and moved on.

He went through the town once more, checking buildings and all other possible hiding places, satisfying himself that no one else remained. It was an eerie sight, these three blocks of renovated town, all the lights blazing, taped music still coming through the windows of the casino and bar. An empty town, all the people gone, as though stricken by a plague. In the distance, he could hear more gunshots, then quiet. The Patrol and police had evidently finished their work. He held the tiny watch-transmitter close to his mouth and spoke into it.

"Calling Colonel Weeks. Do you receive me, Colonel Weeks? Over."

A faint voice replied.

"Colonel Weeks here. Receiving you. Over."

"What is the situation outside the walls? Over."

"Under control, sir. Are you in the town?"

"I am. The town is empty. Two men escaped along the coast. My guess is they headed east through the swamp. One was called Pretty, as in pretty girl. A killer. Another from here went with him, a black. Check the records to identify them, then alert border guards. Over."

"Anything else, sir? Over."

"The body of Matthew Crumb is on the porch of the inn. Send in a detail in the morning. I suggest he be buried in front of the inn. Over."

"Sir, what will happen to this place now? Over."

"I have an idea about that. First, search the records tomorrow to see if Crumb had any heirs. Over."

"Right away. Anything else, sir?"

"One more thing, Colonel. In ten minutes, come into the town yourself with two men. Go to the big building with the sign. Killer Hilton."

"Killer Hilton?" said the Colonel, interrupting.

"Yes, Colonel. On the top floor, there is a large safe. Remove the contents. All stolen property. Understood? Over."

"Understood. Sir, may I ask? How did you do it all? Over."

"All what, Colonel? Over."

"Sorry. Silly question. Sir, I have no words, no words"— the faint voice paused for a moment—"to thank you for my daughter, Caroline. Over."

"Is she all right, Colonel? Over."

"Sleeping like a baby when I left. Over."

"Good."

"Sir, may I ask one more question? Will we ever meet? Sir, are you still receiving me? Over."

There was no answer.

The small Mawitaan jail and the few cells at Jungle Patrol headquarters were crowded with the former citizens of Killer's Town. The town rocked with excitement. Newsmen and TV crews from America and Europe poured into the tropical capital. Three dozen vicious criminals, some escapees from prisons, all of them on the "most wanted" lists in their home countries, all bagged together in one roundup, one of the biggest shootouts in the history of the perpetual battle between crime and law. Fingerprints flew around the world as the prisoners were identified and deported to authorities in their homelands. Some of these authorities were more annoyed than grateful, having hoped to be rid of them. When lists were finally complete, a few of the Killer's Town citizenry were not in hand. The bank robber, Frenchy, was found dead in the town. A few others had been downed in the battle. Among them, Killer Koy himself, said to have been shot in the back by one of his own men, a wild killer called "Pretty," wanted in the States for several especially vicious murders.

The town gave a collective sigh of relief when the last of the captured Killer's Town crowd, wearing handcuffs, was shipped out at the airport under the watchful eyes of Colonel Weeks and Chief Togando. The populace was advised to be on the lookout for two of the criminals who were still at large, a foreigner named Pretty (some name for a killer) and a local named Moogar, an Oogaan boy who had gone bad. Wanted signs for the two were posted, offering a large reward. Now that the criminals were gone, crowds went out to have a look at the fabulous Killer's Town. Though the warehouse and wharf had burned down, the remainder was intact. They could only peer through the gates, and from the high branches of trees outside the wall, as the Patrol permitted no one to enter. All wondered what was to become of the place?

Town Hall records at Mawitaan, including an old lawsuit, proved that Matthew Crumb had no living heirs. The authorities had been assured, by an unknown but unimpeachable source, that no one related to Killer Koy had any claim to the place. Then who had? That question was soon answered.

Several miles inside the jungle, there was a cluster of low buildings, the jungle hospital of Dr. Axel. The doctor had built this place thirty years before as a young man. It was the only modern medicine available to jungle folk, and they waited patiently, sometimes for days to see the beloved doctor. Though there were occasional bandits in the area and no guards in the hospital, no one dared attack or rob the complex. For on the gateposts on either side of the main gate was an odd symbol that looked like two crossed sabers. Or the symbol might have been crossed "P's." No one was certain. But everyone in the jungle knew what it meant. This was the good mark of the Phantom. Wherever it appeared, it meant that place or person was under the protection of the Phantom. Only the most foolish, ignorant, or desperate of men would violate it.

This night, while Dr. Axel relaxed after his usual tiring day, reading Shakespeare by lamplight (the sonnets this time), there was a knock on his shuttered window. Most unusual. He opened the shutters and peered out. A figure loomed in the darkness. At first glance, it seemed gigantic. Then, as his eyes became more accustomed to the dark, he could make out a rider on a white horse. The horse moved slightly. Light from the kerosene lamp touched the figure. Dr. Axel gasped in surprise. He had not seen him in—how many years?

Their relationship had a long history. As a young man, Dr. Axel had first seen this awesome figure when he had been brought blindfolded by the pygmy poison people to a strange place in the Deep Woods. There he had assisted at the birth of a baby in a cave, the strange figure's son. Later, the strange figure had helped him build his first hospital. Still later, he had come to the hospital seriously wounded. Dr. Axel always believed those wounds were fatal. Yet, here was the man again, so many years later! Dr. Axel didn't know, hadn't guessed, that the baby he had helped to deliver in the cave was now the figure on the white horse. And the man he had first seen long ago was this man's father, now dead. All Dr. Axel knew was that this was the Phantom.

Through the years, Dr. Axel had heard a good deal about this Phantom from his jungle patients. The Ghost Who Walks—{he Man Who Cannot Die. With the strength of ten tigers, and the wisdom of the ages. The fabulous Skull Throne. The Skull Cave with its fantastic treasures. Feared by evildoers, loved by good people, the Keeper of the Peace. What does one say in the middle of the night to a man of mystery, to a legend?

"Hello," said Dr. Axel. "How are you?"

It was a question that appeared to need no answer. The man radiated health and power. The question was not answered. Instead. . . .

"Dr. Axel, the coastal tribes, the Mori, the Llongo, and others have always lacked good medical care. This hospital is too far for them."

"True," said Dr. Axel, feeling slightly confused. Had this man of mystery ridden out of the night to tell him this?

"There is a place called Killer's Town, formerly New Metropolis, about forty miles south of Mawitaan. It has three city blocks of new one-story buildings, perfect for staff rooms, clinics, and schools. It has a four-story, forty-seven-room modern inn, perfect for a branch hospital. All the utilities are in—electric power, water. It is well furnished with beds, modern plumbing. You might even call it luxurious. Do you want it for a branch hospital?"

Dr. Axel's head reeled. As the Phantom had described it, he had visualized it and was thinking, What a place for a hospital complex!

"Do I want it? Is this possible?" he stammered.

"I would not be here otherwise. This is the best possible use of that place for the jungle people."

In his years of daily emergencies and makeshift equipment, Dr. Axel had learned to make quick decisions.

"Yes," he said.

"The place is in the custody of the Jungle Patrol. Go to Colonel Weeks's office tomorrow to sign the papers. He is expecting you."

The meeting was over. The big white stallion wheeled about to go.

"I read about that place. Did they get all those men?" asked Dr. Axel.

"All except two. A black and a white. Killers. Their pictures are posted. If any of your people see them, report to the Patrol at once."

The Phantom looked back over his shoulder. His white teeth gleamed in the pale light as he smiled.

"By the way, Dr. Axel. I feel fine."

"Wait," said Dr. Axel, suddenly brimming with a dozen questions. But the white stallion was already gone in the darkness.

"Thank you," Dr. Axel shouted into the night.

CHAPTER 14

"Another swamp!"

"The last one, Pretty. We're almost out."

"Out where? Where you taking us, you jungle bunny?"

Moogar grinned as they sloshed on through the muck, not knowing he was being insulted.

"We've been going in a big circle. The law saw us headin' north on the coast. Now we've moved south, then east."

"Sounds okay," Pretty grunted. They sloshed on. The muck was calf-deep, knee-deep in some places. There was always danger of quicksand. It was hard going. Both men were heavily armed, a rifle, two pistols, and ammunition they'd taken from Killer's Town. The swamp was hot, fetid, filled with mosquitoes and worrisome gnats. An occasional big snake coiled on a branch, startling city-boy Pretty. He shot the first one he saw, a fifteen-foot boa as thick as his thigh. Moogar shouted at him for that.

"You fool," he shouted. "That noise goes for miles. You want the Patrol to find us?"

Pretty grumbled. He made no reply, knowing Moogar was right. But he was ashamed to admit that wild life, especially a big snake, scared him.

Finally, they walked on dry grass and sank down beside a tree, covered with sticky mud to their knees. Both were exhausted.

"That was rough. But we made it. No more swamps," said Moogar.

Pretty nodded. He grumbled for a few minutes about the lost treasures in Roy's safe—as he did every few hours. Then they both fell asleep. They were awakened a few hours after dawn by a pounding sound.

"What's that?" mumbled Pretty. "Some damn animal?"

"Shh," said Moogar quickly, sitting up and listening alertly.

"Yes, some damn animal. A man," he chuckled. He had his own sense of humor.

Both men checked their rifles, then moved toward file pounding noise. Moogar grasped Pretty's arm, motioning him to the ground. They crawled on hands and knees to a thick clump of bushes and cautiously peered over them.

There was a clearing ahead, a dirt road. On it, the well-known small open vehicle with large letters painted on the side: Jungle Patrol. Near the car, a uniformed patrolman was nailing a placard on a big tree.

"Is that a cop?" said Pretty, looking at the pith helmet and shorts.

"More like ten cops," whispered Moogar. "Patrol. Tough."

Pretty nodded, grinned, and, before Moogar realized it, raised his rifle and fired. But in the split second before firing, Moogar grabbed Pretty's arm, jolting him. The patrolman fell with a surprised cry, shot in the back. Pretty turned to Moogar, his eyes blazing.

"You bastard," he swore. "Almost made me miss."

Moogar glared back at him. "You crazy, shooting a jungle patrolman? Those guys are murder."

They watched for a moment. The fallen man did not move. There was no one else there. They walked into the clearing. The man lay quietly, a red blotch showing through his shirt. It wasn't apparent whether he was breathing or not. They looked at the sign on the tree. Moogar gasped. Pretty laughed. The placard was about them. It had prison photos of both of them full face and profile, height, weight, coloring, distinguishing marks, with the remarks: "Known to be armed. Both are killers. Reward."

"How about that? Only a ten-grand reward for each of us? Are they kidding? Cheapskates," said Pretty, laughing.

Moogar pulled the placard from the tree and tore it into pieces. He had the jungleman's superstitious fear of photographs of himself. There was a loud buzzing from the car. They rushed over to it.

"It's the radio," said Pretty, grinning as he lifted the radio-telephone from the hook on the dashboard. A voice came out of the loudspeaker.

"Calling JP 604. Calling JP 604. Come in—" The voice dissolved into static. Pretty pointed to the hood. The number 604 was marked there. Pretty grinned and uttered a string of obscenities into the receiver not knowing if his words were being transmitted, but enjoying the gesture. Then Moogar looked at the sky in alarm. His jungle-trained ears had heard something.

"What?" asked Pretty.

Moogar pointed to a cloud. At that moment, a craft, like some gigantic mosquito, sailed out of the clouds-—a helicopter. The two men stared up at it.

In the helicopter, five hundred feet up, the radio patrolman repeated his call. "Calling JP 604. Calling JP 604. No answer yet. 604 should be in this area. We're over the Phantom Trail now." He looked down through powerful binoculars.

"Hey, I think I see the car. Yes, there it is. Lower." The helicopter dropped a hundred feet. Through the binoculars, he could see the car clearly now. There was a figure lying on the road, a man. Two men standing near, looking up.

"Hey, I think that's Sandy down there."

On the ground, Moogar grabbed Pretty's arm.

"They see us."

They both moved off the road into the bushes at the side.

"That guy's still breathing," said Pretty, aiming his rifle at the prone patrolman. This time Moogar grabbed Pretty's arm and pulled him violently into the bushes.

"In the jungle we kill when we have to," he said angrily. Pretty pulled his arm away, and glared at Moogar. The black's muscles bulged. He had the build of a welterweight. A tough jungle man. He was facing up to Pretty, unafraid. At that moment, a blast hit only a few yards from them. Machine-gun fire from the helicopter. They'd been spotted.

"I'll take care of you later," muttered Pretty under his breath as the two dashed into the woods.

The craft hovered over the clearing like a giant insect, then landed lightly and delicately, the wind from its whirling props waving the grass and ferns and raising the dust of the road. Concealed in the bushes, Pretty and Moogar watched the landing. Pretty raised his rifle, showing his teeth in his wolflike grin.

"I can get those guys from here," he said. "Blow up that thing." Again Moogar stopped him.

"You crazy? They got a machine gun," he whispered tensely. Pretty shrugged and lowered his rifle. They crouched and watched and waited.

The two patrolmen, guns in hand, leaped from the helicopter, looked about quickly, then ran to the fallen patrolman.

"It's Sandy. Shot in the back. Still breathing."

The pilot ran back to the craft, and pulled out an emergency stretcher, part of their standard equipment. Meanwhile, the other man. Sergeant Tamos, cut off the shirt and applied first aid to the wound.

"He's lucky. Looks like it just missed his heart and lungs."

Sandy, half-conscious now, heard that as they lifted him carefully on the stretcher.

"Always lucky," he said thickly. "Like the time I broke a leg instead of my back."

"Quiet, save your strength," said Tamos.

But Sandy chattered on, his words fuzzy because of the morphine they'd given him.

"Shot in the back, putting up the sign."

"Did you see them, Sandy?"

"No, shot in the back."

They lifted him carefully into the plane.

"Guess we know who did it," said Tamos, holding up the torn pieces of the placard.

"Should we have a look around?"

"No. Got to get him back to the hospital."

Pretty and Moogar watched the craft lift off and disappear beyond the treetops. Then they ran to the car.

"How about that! They left the key," said Pretty.

"They figure nobody's dumb enough to steal a Patrol car," said Moogar. Pretty grinned at him as he climbed in the driver's seat, his animosity toward the black man forgotten in this stroke of luck.

"Nobody but me. Where's this road go?" he asked as they bumped along the dirt trail.

"To Obano. Little town."

"That's for us."

"Man, we got to hide. They probably got our pictures all over."

"They got stores in this town?"

"One store. Pretty, we got to hide out. The Patrol'll be hot after us."

"Hide out. Sure," said Pretty, getting irritable. "But first we need supplies. Food, ammo. Got it?"

Moogar nodded, realizing Pretty was determined. Jungle-bred, Moogar could live on what the jungle offered. But if things got tough, perhaps Pretty couldn't handle a diet of grubs and roots. He grinned at the thought.

They drove into Obano, a jungle town of a few hundred people that served as a marketplace and caravan stop. There was one general store, a trading post, where jungle folk bartered garden crops, animal skins, and handicraft objects for such things as cloth, salt, matches, axes eyeglasses (without prescriptions), and other products of civilization. The town consisted of a main street with several dozen wooden shacks with roofs of palm fronds. The dirt street was wide and dusty, and at this midday hour, hot and almost deserted. A few naked children played in the dust. Their elders were asleep inside. It was siesta time. Moogar gasped and pointed as they drove slowly along this street. The "wanted" placard bearing their photographs was posted on a tree. The Patrol had already been there, perhaps the same patrolman Pretty had shot in the woods.

"So what," said Pretty. But he drove with one hand, holding a gun in the other. "Where's that store?"

Moogar pointed to one shack larger than the rest. Instead of a palm-frond roof, it had tarpaper. "Pretty, we got no money," he said, as they stopped in front of the store.

"Who needs money?" said Pretty, grinning. "Come on, I need you to talk this jerky jungle talk."

As they walked into the store, the little naked children ran toward them, attracted by the unusual sight of the car and a white man.

The proprietor, a middle-aged bald black man, was dozing in an old battered canvas steamer chair set amidst bins of vegetables. He wore trousers, an apron, and was barefoot. A little radio on the floor near him was playing soft recorded music from the Mawitaan station. Pretty, grinning, started to pull out the rear support so that the steamer chair would flatten out, dumping the sleeping man on the floor. But Moogar restrained him and shook the man's shoulder. He awoke with a start at the sight of the two strangers.

"Tell him we're Jungle Patrol," said Pretty.

Moogar translated, pointing to the vehicle outside, and told him what they wanted. Food, ammunition, tobacco, oil, gasoline. The man rubbed his eyes and got up wearily, looking at them and at the car that bore the large letters: JUNGLE PATROL. A car like that had been in the village recently. Patrolmen weren't seen here often. The town was actually beyond their jurisdiction. But when they did come, they didn't look like these two. They wore crisp uniforms and helmets, and were clean-shaven and clean. These two were neither. They were caked with dried swamp mud, both had several days' growth of beard and, it was obvious to his sensitive nose, neither had bathed in a long time. Somehow, they looked familiar. Whoever they were, he was sure they weren't Jungle Patrol. What did it matter? A customer was a customer.

He began filling the order, loading two crates. As he reached for soap and salt, he noticed the placard that had recently been posted on the wall by a patrolman. His heart skipped a beat.

With the heavy crate in his arms, he turned slowly to face the two men. The black looked troubled. The white was grinning.

"This will cost forty," he said, his voice trembling. The black translated to the white. The white said something in his incomprehensible tongue. The black translated.

"Carry it to the car."

"First my money."

The black translated. The white took a gun from his belt and pointed it at the man. There was no need for translation. Sweating, the man started for the car. Music from the radio stopped abruptly. A voice came on with an announcement in the Bangalla tongue.

". . . two escaped killers, armed and dangerous, last seen on the Phantom Trail near Obano. Names are Pretty and Moogar, a white American and black from the tribe of Oogaan. If you see them, report to Jungle Patrol at once." Then music.

Pretty watched suspiciously, noting the tension of both blacks during the announcement. The storekeeper's eyes rolled with fear and he began to breathe hard. Moogar translated quickly for Pretty.

Outside the store, the man stopped, the crate in his arms. The little naked children stood near, their eyes wide at the sight of the strangers.

"I want my money," he said.

Moogar translated for Pretty. Pretty waved the gun at the man, indicating to him to put the box in the car. He did, then turned defiantly to Moogar.

"You're the ones they're looking for," he shouted, Moogar translating.

"Ain't he the bright one?" said Pretty.

"I'm a poor man. You are robbing me. You can't get away with this. I will report you," he shouted, shaking his fist a foot from Pretty's nose, and in his rage ignoring the gun. Pretty's grin remained as he fired straight into the man's chest. The storekeeper clutched himself, then dropped to the ground. At the sound of the shot, the children screamed and began running.

"You fool!" shouted Moogar. "You didn't have to do that!"

Pretty's smile was gone. The wild light danced in his eyes.

"Get the other box. Move!" he said. "And bring that radio."

Moogar hesitated. His own gun was in his belt. Then he turned quickly, picked up the other loaded crate and radio and placed them in the back seat with the first crate. Pretty had started the car, and it was moving. Moogar had to run to jump in. Some of the men and women in the shacks, hearing the shot and the children's cries appeared in doorways and peered from windows. Their voices began to rise as the car roared through the short street and disappeared around a bend on the Phantom Trail into the jungle.

The car raced over the rough trail for a time, jolting over roots and bumps, then, satisfied they weren't being followed, continued at a slower speed. They drove on in silence for a while.

"That was a stupid thing to do," said Moogar. "Now you'll have the Jungle Patrol after us."

"Are you kiddin'? They're already after us."

"Now they know where we are. You didn't have to shoot that man. He was not armed. Why did you do it?"

"Because I wanted to," said Pretty quietly, his eyes on the road. He seemed satisfied, like a man after a full meal.

Moogar sat quietly, thinking about those words "because I wanted to." He had had his share of violence. He had drifted into crime as a youth, and remained stuck in it. Fights, assaults, jail cells. But his people, the small peaceful tribe of Oogaan, believed in the sanctity of human life and in their ancestor worship regarded the immortal human soul as sacred. An Oogaan did not kill, except in a fit of passion or in self-defense. What kind of man was this white, this Pretty? he wondered. He would learn shortly, if he hadn't already learned enough.

"Where does this road go?" asked Pretty after a few miles of twisting and bouncing.

"Another few miles. Then it ends, at The Canyon of The Ghost Who Walks."

"That's the name of a canyon?"

"It is."

"What a lousy name. This road, what did you call it?"

"Phantom Trail."

"Is that the same as the spook you kept talking about?" Moogar nodded. He resented the use of that word "spook." It sounded like a put-down. Though neither he nor anyone he knew had ever seen the Phantom, he respected the legendary figure as did all his people. Pretty grinned.

"Phantom—Ghost Who Walks. What a bunch of weirdos."

The trail ended in an abrupt roadblock made of big boulders. Beyond, there was a steep cliff bordering a canyon, five-hundred feet deep at this point, filled with crags, towers, battlements, brown, red, purple—carved through the centuries by the silver stream that wound among the trees and rocks far below. A smaller version of the Grand Canyon in the United States.

The two men unloaded the supplies then, at Pretty's direction, rolled the car to the edge of the cliff. Moogar was puzzled.

"Why are we doing that?"

Pretty did not answer. He was busy pouring a can of gasoline over the car. Then he turned on the ignition and let the motor idle.

"What are you doing, Pretty?" demanded Moogar.

"Don't ask so many questions, stupid. Just push," he said. Together the two shoved the car. It rolled over the edge and dropped into the depths. Pretty quickly fired a shot at the gas tank. There was a small explosion, then flames leaped about the car. In another moment, the car hit bottom with a crash and a big explosion. It was hidden in flames. Moogar stared. "Pretty, why did you-----?" he began.

"Don't you get it? When the Jungle Patrol comes lookin' for us, like you keep sayin' they will, they'll think we're down there, dead. Get it, stupid?"

"Don't call me stupid," said Moogar angrily.

"Okay genius. Now what? Into the woods?"

"There is no other way," said Moogar, annoyed with Pretty but realizing he'd done a clever thing.

"We can't carry these crates," said Pretty.

"These knapsacks were in the car. We can use them."

They transferred the essential supplies into the knapsacks. As they started off the trail into the woods, an antelope broke cover and leaped across the road. That was a mistake. Pretty jerked his rifle to his shoulder and fired. The animal fell to the trail, writhed a moment, then was quiet. Dead. Moogar glared at Pretty.

"Why did you do that?"

"We're miles from anybody. Nobody can hear," said Pretty.

"I don't mean that," said Moogar. "We can't carry that doe. Too big."

"Carry it? You kiddin'? Who wants to carry it?" said Pretty.

"You want to eat it here?"

"You losin' your marbles? We got to move."

"Then why did you shoot it?"

Pretty grinned at him, and for a moment the wild light danced in his eyes. "Because I wanted to," he said.

They walked off through the bushes into the woods. Behind, on the Phantom Trail, the dead fawn was already attracting a host of flies and ants. Larger scavengers would soon arrive by air and land. And far below, the wreck of the car blazed at the bottom of the Canyon of The Ghost Who Walks.

CHAPTER 15

In Jungle Patrol headquarters. Sergeant Tamos stood at ease before Colonel Weeks.

"Report of a robbery and shooting at Obano yesterday. Those may be our men, Sergeant."

"I hope so, sir. I am most anxious to put my hands on the one who shot Sandy in the back". Tamos spoke with a slight accent. He had come all the way from Crete to join the Patrol. "What's the latest news on Sandy, sir?"

"Doc says he'll be okay. Narrow escape. If that bullet had been a quarter-inch over, he'd be paralyzed for life."

"Thank God," said Tamos.

"Take Morgan with you. Tamos. Check the area. Try to find those two." He held up the "Wanted" placard that had the photos and descriptions of Pretty and Moogar. "Be careful. They're both tough. From what we know, this one —Pretty—is a cold-blooded killer."

"Yes sir," said Tamos. He saluted and went to the door, then turned back.

"Thanks for this assignment, sir. Sandy's my buddy."

"I know, Sergeant."

The helicopter dropped out of the sky on the broad lawn in front of Dr. Axel's jungle hospital. Patients and white-clad doctors and nurses leaned out of the windows, and thronged on the broad veranda to watch the landing. Morgan and Tamos went quickly to the office of Dr. Axel who was expecting them, having been advised by radio of their coming.

"The man from Obano is in critical condition, but he is conscious, able to talk," said Dr. Axel as he led them through the corridor. The wounded storekeeper had been brought on a crude stretcher by his neighbors who carried him half a day and all night to reach the hospital. At the bedside, Tamos held up the placard. The man, wrapped in white bandages, partially sedated, looked at him with dull, sick eyes that suddenly blazed.

"Know these men, Mr. Muzzas?"

"Yes. Those are the ones. They robbed me. That one"— he pointed a finger weakly at Pretty—"that one shot me."

"What else can you tell us about them?" said Tamos. The man muttered and coughed.

"I'm afraid that must be enough questions for now," said Dr. Axel. But as the patrolmen reached the door, the man called after them with sudden vigor.

"Find them. They took my radio."

The patrolmen nodded and left. That battery radio was probably the only one in the village. Their next stop was at Obano. The helicopter dropped onto the wide main street, raising plumes of dust and scattering squawking chickens and shouting children. The villagers converged on the patrolmen at the side of the craft and, in answer to their questions about the robbers, pointed down the road. Two husky young men, sons of the storekeeper, begged to go along, and bravely entered the helicopter before the admiring gazes of their relatives and neighbors. Neither had ever flown before, but after their first moment of terror, anger against their father's attackers overcame their fear.

The helicopter sailed over the treetops, following the Phantom Trail below. They continued to the end, where the trail dropped off into the canyon. They circled for a few minutes, then Morgan spotted the wreckage. They dropped down as far as they dared, among the sheer walls of the canyon, examining the twisted, blackened wreckage with binoculars. There was no sign of bodies. On the hood, still partially readable, were the numbers 604.

"That's Sandy's buggy all right," said Tamos.

"They were barreling along. Didn't know the road," said Morgan.

"A lousy way to go, even for those two," he added.

"I don't know," said Tamos, Sandy's buddy. "They had it all coming."

He talked into his microphone, transmitting back to Patrol H.Q. He spoke directly with Colonel Weeks.

"The car obviously fell to the bottom, maybe five hundred feet, exploded, and burned. Anybody in that car is dead. We can't land close enough to examine the wreck, sir. Over."

"Return to Obano. Form a search party to go down on foot for a final look. It would appear the fugitives are dead. Over."

The Mawitaan radio station carried the news bulletin.

"Escaped killers believed dead in jungle accident, according to a report from the Jungle Patrol. The burned wreckage was spotted from the air. The fugitives, Moogar of Oogaan and a foreign gangster nicknamed Pretty, were the last survivors of the infamous Killer's Town, which will soon be converted to a hospital."

The radio broadcast was received in many places, as well as at Colonel Weeks's table as he was dining with Caroline.

"That's wonderful," she said. "I remember that Pretty. He was a monster."

"We think they're dead. Not positive yet," said Weeks.

"When will you be positive?"

"A search party's climbing into the canyon to examine the wreck."

Somewhere east of the canyon, in deep jungle, Pretty and Moogar sat at a campfire roasting a rabbit Moogar had snared. The radio was on a stump near them. They heard the news. Both men shouted with relief.

"The killers are dead. Hey, that's us!" yelled Pretty. "Didn't I tell you? They fell for it!"

Farther east, in an inaccessible part of the jungle, the Deep Woods, the Phantom sat beside his radio in a rocky chamber inside the Skull Cave. Devil, the mountain wolf, lay at his feet. The Phantom had followed the news broadcasts since returning. These were the two who had shot old Matthew Crumb. The first bulletin announced the shooting of Patrolman Sandy Dunker and the theft of his car. The next announcement told of the robbery and shooting at the general store in Obano. Now this—dead in a car wreck at the bottom of the canyon. Was there positive proof they'd died in the crash? One, or both might have survived, jumped out in time or fallen free. He knew the area well. He pictured the end of the trail at that point, the pile of boulders that formed the roadblock. Impossible not to see that. Possible, with some effort, to drive around them. Could the fall, the crash, not have been accidental, but planned? A search party was going there on foot. He would wait for more news.

Seated at their campfire, Pretty and Moogar were having their after-dinner coffee when they heard the next radio bulletin.

". . . and a local team headed by the Jungle Patrol's Sergeant Tamos is descending into the canyon to retrieve the bodies of the fugitives. It is a difficult climb down the steep sides of this little-known canyon. Word should be received soon when they report the findings." Music continued. Pretty laughed.

"Hey, that's good. Maybe we can go to our own funeral."

"How about when they go down there and find we're not there?" said Moogar.

"In that explosion, we coulda been blown into seven countries. Let them look. They can't find anything. Our trail's cold."

There was a rustle in the bushes, Pretty sat up quickly, rifle in hand. The weapon never left his side. Moogar remained relaxed. He knew the sound of a little animal. A little animal it was, an ordinary house cat, a big tom that had probably wandered away from a village. It moved across the clearing stealthily, like a miniature tiger. Pretty fired. The heavy-caliber blast tore the small animal apart. Moogar sat up in surprise. The shot caused movement and chattering in the branches around as monkeys and birds moved in the foliage. Pretty shot again. There was a shower of bright feathers, all that was left of a parrot. A split second later, another shot. A small brown monkey fell onto the ground. Moogar jumped to his feet.

"You wild-----!" he said. "You got to kill everything that moves?"

"You bother me," said Pretty, holding the smoking rifle. "Want to make something out of it?"

"No," he said, looking at the grim face of the killer. This is how he thought of Pretty now, the killer. He's crazy, a nut, he told himself, using an expression he'd heard Pretty use. I'll shake him when I can.

Pretty sat on a boulder near the radio and looked at Moogar's broad back. I hate these woods, and I hate this jungle creep, he thought. But I need him in here. As soon as I get out, I'll finish him.

They both slept poorly that night, both trying to keep one eye open to watch each other. They fell asleep through sheer exhaustion. Both awoke in the morning, delighted that nothing had happened. After coffee, bacon, and cigarettes, they shouldered their packs and moved on.

"Moogar, where's this place we're going?"

"A place for old people."

"An old folks' home? Are you kidding?"

"Not a home. More like a town. A village."

As the two trudged through the thick underbrush—there was no path—Moogar explained. In the olden times, the tribes put their old folks out in the woods for the big cats to eat.

"Before they were dead?" asked Pretty.

"Yes. That's how they got rid of them."

"A good idea," pronounced Pretty.

"Then the Phantom stopped that, and started this village where the old folks could go to live out their last years. They can't work so all the tribes bring food and what they need."

"Phantom. Is that the same spook Killer tried to bluff us with? Moogar, you don't really believe it way down. Do you?"

Moogar was tired of the old argument.

"Believe what you like. Just pray you never meet him."

"I won't hold my breath till I do, either. How much farther to this old folks' place?"

"A day and a night."

A day and a night more of these woods? It was impossible to see more than ten feet in any directions. They had to struggle for every foot through thick thorny bushes. They needed big knives, machetes, to clear the way. They had none. So they trudged and struggled on. There were fleas and mosquitoes, scorpions, spiders as big as dinner plates, snakes, and an occasional big animal rustling in the bushes. At night glowing eyes. Strange cries and howls. Pretty suddenly felt grateful for stolid Moogar, thankful he hadn't already shot him.

"Lonesome out here. Good to be with a pal," he said.

Moogar's thoughts were interrupted. First chance I get to ditch this crazy killer, I'll take off, he thought

"Yeah," he said aloud.

The search party—Sergeant Tamos and the two sons of the storekeeper—reached the wreck at the bottom of the Canyon of the Ghost Who Walks. It had been dangerous, climbing down. Each had slipped many times. There had been too narrow escapes from plunging to death. But now they were down there. High above, the helicopter hovered, watching them, watching the surrounding area for men or animals. The team carefully searched the wreck which was cold by now. They searched the area for hundreds of yards on both sides. They searched the swift little river, the trees and bushes. They looked into every possible and conceivable place. They wanted to find the bodies. These were the men who had shot Sandy in the back, who had robbed and critically wounded their father. But there was no trace of the fugitives. Not a thread, not a bloodstain. Nothing.

Using his walkie-talkie. Tamos contacted the helicopter above.

"No soap, Morgan," he said. "Nothing here. But nothing. The supplies they stole—no trace. No guns, no ammo, nothing. My guess is they weren't in the car when it went over."

"Pushed it over? Faked it?"

"Could be. Just send word back. May still be at large. Morgan, we'll climb out now. Meet us back at the village. Over."

"This is terrible," said Colonel Weeks. "We told everyone they were dead. Get the word out at once—they may be alive." The news bulletin followed swiftly on the Mawitaan radio.

"The two fugitives, Pretty and Moogar, are now believed to be alive, according to the Jungle Patrol. A search of their wrecked vehicle revealed no trace of the killers. Everyone in the area east of Obano is warned to be on the lookout. These two men are dangerous and armed. If you see them, report to the Jungle Patrol at once."

Colonel Weeks listened gloomily to the news broadcast.

"One slight problem," he said. "Our jurisdiction doesn't extend as far as Obano, much less east of it."

"Who is the law east of Obano?" asked Caroline.

"That's the joker in the deck. There is no law. Only the local tribes who manage their own affairs. They'd have no concern about fugitives like these unless they disturbed their village. Which I'm sure these two won't do. That's why they went that way. One of them is a jungle man. He knows they're safe there."

"That's terrible," said Caroline. "You mean, nobody can go after those two who shot Sandy and that old man?"

Weeks's staff at the Jungle Patrol had the same reaction.

"What if it is beyond our legal jurisdiction?" said Captain Smyth. "No one—but no one—will object if we send a posse after them."

The others agreed. Weeks shook his head.

"Our charter is precise and definite about our area," he said.

"Okay. Suppose we go on our own? A private hunting party," said Smyth.

Weeks considered that. Like his men, he was loath to give up the search for the desperadoes. At that moment, a call came on his desk phone.

"The X band," said the excited voice of the radio operator.

"Excuse me, men," said Weeks. The men filed out. They'd heard the magic words "X band." All knew what that meant. The Commander. Somehow, when things became crucial, he was always in touch. How did he always know?

The same thought went through Weeks's head as he answered the phone.

"Weeks here," he said.

"What did they find in the wreck out there. Colonel?" said the familiar deep voice, wasting no time on small talk. Weeks told him.

"You believe the men are alive?"

"Sergeant Tamos does and he was on the spot. He believes they faked the accident. My men are anxious to go after them. As you know, it's beyond our jurisdiction."

"True, Colonel."

"What'll we do?"

"Nothing."

"Nothing? Sir, my men have a plan to go out as a private hunting party, off-duty so to speak."

"Interesting idea. But no, Colonel. The original plans for the Patrol control area were drawn up to protect the deep jungle people from all outside interference. That includes the Patrol," said the voice with an amused laugh.

"I understand. What are our orders?"

"Do no more in this case. I will take over. Understood?"

"You will take over. Er—sir?"

"Yes, Colonel."

"These are bad ones. Particularly that Pretty—a coldblooded killer."

"I know. He shot old Matthew Crumb. Anything else, Colonel?"

"No sir."

The connection clicked off. Somewhere, a phone receiver had been hung up. Matthew Crumb? How did the Commander know that? How did he know everything? Where was he? What was he? Who was he? Blast!

CHAPTER 16

Trader Ed was one of the last of a vanishing breed of wandering merchants who carried their entire stock of merchandise on the back of a donkey. No one, including Ed, knew exactly how old he was. Some said sixty. Some said eighty. He had walked the jungle trails for decades, bartering his goods—costume jewelry, medicines, everyday hardware like needles, pins, scissors and knives, a few utensils, recently a few small battery radios. It was Ed's boast that he could go anywhere in the jungle and be welcomed, even by the savage Tirangi (headhunters, off and on) and the Massagni (cannibals, now and then). Only the shadowy land of the pygmy Bandar, the Deep Woods, was out of bounds for him. He was known and liked by all jungle folk, because he was a fair trader, a friendly man, and spoke most of the jungle dialects.

Old Ed was mostly white. He had always claimed one Eskimo grandmother, an exotic race that had never been seen in this jungle, which was probably why he had chosen it. He had no fear of jungle animals, always having been a good hunter and accurate shot. Besides, he knew that most jungle animals, including the big cats, preferred to flee rather than fight unless cornered. He'd had one or two narrow escapes with cats that didn't flee, and he bore his many scars proudly. He had an endless stream of yarns and anecdotes, and could joke in a dozen languages. In any time or place, Ed would be considered a rare character. And though surrounded by many kinds of possible dangers throughout his career, he'd led a charmed life . . . up to this day.

The Mawitaan radio broadcast the news bulletin: "The Jungle Patrol announced today they'd abandoned the search for the two fugitives from Killer's Town, believed to be in deep jungle somewhere east of Obano. No reason was given for the decision." The daily Mawitaan Times carried the same story. Newsmen and indignant citizens besieged Colonel Weeks with questions. Why? His only answer was, "A policy decision." To inquiries from the Citizens Council, he told one truth: the area was outside Jungle Patrol jurisdiction. The Patrol was never eager to advertise the limits of its authority. It might give lawbreakers too many ideas about where they could find a refuge outside the law.

Two lawbreakers were aware of that. As they stopped in a clearing for coffee and cigarettes, Pretty and Moogar turned on their little radio, stolen from the storekeeper of Obano. They were jubilant when they heard the announcement.

"Abandoned the search for us?" said Moogar.

"That means they quit, gave up," said Pretty smugly.

"I know what it means," snapped Moogar. "They don't come this far anyhow. Everybody in the jungle knows that."

"We're outside the law. Right? All law," said Pretty.

"More or less."

"What do you mean, more or less?"

"We stopped here because I saw something I want to show you," said Moogar.

Pretty looked around the clearing at the bushes and trees. "Saw what?"

"On that big tree," said Moogar, pointing to it.

"What about it?"

Moogar got up and walked to it, then motioned to Pretty to join him. "This," he said, pointing to a mark on the tree.

A circle about a foot in diameter had been cut, about an inch deep into the wood. In the circle, a symbol was clearly carved. It looked like crossed sabers, or perhaps crossed P's.

"So what is it?" said Pretty.

"Good mark of Phantom. It means this part of the jungle is under Phantom peace," explained Moogar defiantly, trying to ignore Pretty's sarcastic expression.

"Phantom again. Yeah, I thought it'd be more hocus-pocus about your spook," said Pretty.

"Phantom peace means there is no war, no fighting, no crime, no killing in this area. It is agreed among tribes," continued Moogar doggedly, trying to convince Pretty.

"No crime? No killing among all you jungle crazies? I'll bet."

"It is true," said Moogar. "For it is written, in the land of the Phantom peace, a beautiful woman may walk alone at midnight wearing precious jewels and not be molested."

Pretty laughed out loud at that. "Just show her to me. I'll molest her!"

Moogar pointed to the mark. "It is not a thing to laugh about. This mark means he will avenge any crime done here."

"I see. You're trying to tell me we're still not outside the law? That your spook is. the law?"

"He is not the law. The people make the Phantom peace. He is a friend of the people," said Moogar, struggling to explain the difficult concept of the Phantom. He'd grown up with it, but had never tried to explain it before.

Pretty laughed. He ground his lighted cigarette into the circle, then stepped back, fired a bullet into the mark.

"That's what I think of your spook, Moogar," he said.

Moogar was startled.

"That was bad to do. That means bad luck!"

Like most outlaws or other men who live constantly on the edge of danger, Pretty was superstitious. Luck was a real thing to him. You needed luck to get through the day, and more especially, the night. Bad luck? A slight tremor of fear went through him. He overcame it with swagger.

"I've heard enough of your yapping about that spook. Phantom this, Phantom that. I don't want to hear any more. Hear?"

"I hear," said Moogar, walking away. He was pleased. He had seen the flicker in Pretty's eyes at the words "bad luck." He turned back. "You keep firing that gun, somebody's going to hear, and come looking."

"There's nobody in this damn jungle but us and the bugs," said Pretty.

A short distance away, beyond a line of trees, Trader Ed was leading Cuddles, his loaded donkey. He paused, surprised at the sound. He had heard the shot. Close by, a real surprise. He didn't know there were any guns in these woods, outside of his. Who was shooting? He moved quietly and peered through the bushes. Two men, walking back to a little campfire, drinking coffee, lighting cigarettes. One white, one black. A memory clicked in Ed's mind. He pulled a placard out of his pack. He'd torn it off a tree far back near Obano. He looked at the photos, then at the two. They were the men. Dangerous armed killers. No place for old Ed. He started to move off quietly with Cuddles. That is hard to do with a donkey. It is difficult to get them to walk on tiptoes, and not to hee-haw. Cuddles hadn't hee-hawed all day. He chose to do it now. Ed groaned and began to move faster. "Shh, Cuddles," he whispered.

"Hey, you," called a voice from the clearing. "What's your hurry?"

Oh, oh, though Trader Ed. This might be tough.

It would be.

The Phantom raced through the jungle on his great white stallion, Hero, with the mountain wolf, Devil, at his heels. He chose hidden paths known only to jungle hunters, and avoided the tribal villages. A few hunters in the woods far from home heard the thundering hooves and knew the sound. There was none other like it in the jungle. And fewer, perhaps three or four, had a glimpse of the big mount and his rider as they sped by on the shadowy paths. Though this might have been their first view of him in their entire lives, all knew who he was. This was a sight they could tell their children and grandchildren about. And in each retelling, the image of rider and horse would become bigger, and their pace would become faster until they were flying above the treetops, faster than the wind. And even if the listeners only half-believed, for they were not foolish but wise, yet it was the kind of tale they loved to hear about their beloved Keeper of the Peace.

He reached the roadblock at the end of the Phantom Trail. He peered into the depths of the canyon of the Ghost Who Walks and saw the blackened wreck far below. Then on foot, followed by Devil who held the ends of Hero's reins in his teeth and so led the white stallion, the Phantom trailed the two fugitives. Their trail was easy to find. They had cut a clear path, leaving trampled grass and broken branches. And a dead antelope. He examined the partly devoured carcass. A hyena and vultures had already been at work. The animal had been killed by a single shot through the head. Why? he wondered. Clearly the work of the fugitives. It seemed pointless. Antelope meat was highly prized, a delicacy. If you shot it, you butchered it and ate it, taking the surplus with you. Meat was not easy to come by. In the jungle, it was not wasted like this.

He continued to follow the trail. Cigarette butts, a few cans and other trash. Then more dead animals, killed by rifle fire. The scattered remains of a parrot. A house cat, obviously someone's pet. A little brown monkey. Further on, a wild pig, more birds, another monkey. Two things were clear. The fugitives were carrying supplies and had no need to hunt food, or they would have eaten some of the game. The other fact that seemed clear was that this was the work of a wanton killer.

In the jungle, only the leopard is known to kill for the pleasure of killing. All other animals, and jungle folk, kill for food or for survival. What had poor Matthew Crumb said? "That one called Pretty. He's the worst of the lot."

The Obano storekeeper had pointed to Pretty's photo as the one who shot him. And some testimony of the Killer's Town captives, corroborating Crumb's story of the death of Killer Koy, had quoted the late ganglord's description of Pretty—"a mad dog killer."

Koy's description of Pretty was like the pot calling the kettle black, thought the Phantom. It takes one to know one. Koy was gone, but the "mad dog" was ahead somewhere. Also, his companion, Moogar. Was he a killer too? Doubtful, since he was of Oogaan. Now the Phantom moved at a fast pace, Hero and Devil following closely. Then, far ahead, there was a faint sound alien to the jungle. It was like a distant clap of hands or a tap. Devil's and Hero's ears stood up alertly. It was gunshot, miles away. Another bird or animal? Or a man this time? The Phantom mounted Hero, and the stallion moved fast, alternating between a walk, trot, and canter, threading his way through the thick underbrush as only a jungle-bred horse could.

Ed stood with Cuddles as the two men approached him. He held the placard behind his back, and cursed himself for not having thrown it away. It was too late now.

"Who's that old crock," said Pretty.

"Old Ed, a trader. Works the villages. Now, Pretty, he's no trouble."

Ed's free hand was resting on the butt of his pistol that was in a holster at his hip. But Pretty's gun was pointing at him.

"Don't go reaching for that, or this one's liable to go off," said Pretty. "What are you doing here?"

"Mindin' my own business," said Ed, his jaws moving on a chaw of tobacco.

"What are you hidin' there?"

"That's my business," said Ed calmly, his sharp eyes searching Pretty's face. He recognized the type. A wild kid. The other one, the black, looked worried. He seemed like a decent sort.

"Don't talk smart with me," said Pretty. "Show it to me."

Old Ed knew he was trapped. These two, hiding from the law, weren't likely to waste much time with him. His only chance was to shoot that gun out of the kid's hand, hit him in the hand or arm.

"Well," he said slowly, launching a squirt of tobacco juice to the side, "I might just------" And he drew his gun as fast as he could. Not fast enough. Pretty's gun exploded. The impact of the bullet felt like Cuddles had kicked him in the stomach. He tottered, then fell to the ground.

"Damn you, Pretty," he heard the black shout, as if from a distance. "Do you have to kill everything?"

He ain't going' to kill me. I ain't goin' to die, thought Ed to himself, keeping his eyes closed.

"What you expect me to do? Let the old crock shoot me? Look at this." Pretty picked up the placard. "Knew who we are. Probably going for the reward."

"Now that's a lie. I'm no cop. Never turned in a man in my life," said Ed, suddenly indignant, his eyes open.

"How about that? The old coot's still kickin'," said Pretty. He aimed his gun at the old man's head, but Moogar stopped him angrily.

"That's enough," he said. "Let him be."

The two glared at each other. Pretty's gun was in his hand. Moogar's was in his holster. Once more the hostility between the two flared into the open. But Ed's husky voice broke the tension.

"I was slow, slow," he moaned. "Twenty years ago I was the fastest gun on the coast."

"Sure you were, pop," said Pretty, laughing.

"Twenty years ago, I woulda put a bullet between your eyes before you knew what hit you."

"Sure you would, pop," said Pretty, returning his gun to his holster. "Let's see what he's got here."

They went through the pack and saddlebags on Cuddles's back, dumping everything on the ground. The costume jewelry and the knives and scissors sparkled in the sun.

"Bunch of trash," said Pretty scornfully. "Leave it."

"No. Good stuff," said Moogar, knowing the value of these things for jungle trading. He stuffed some back into the saddlebags, knives, scissors, costume jewelry, the radios. Also, some food and ammunition. Pretty went through the old man's pockets. Ed watched him silently, unable to resist. Pretty rolled him on his side, as if he were a cadaver, and pulled out a wallet. It contained a pad of money, the equivalent of about a hundred dollars.

"How about this?" said Pretty. "Been cheatin' the jungle bunnies, have you, you old coot?" he said, putting the money in his pocket. Then he removed Ed's gunbelt with the pistol, and threw it over his shoulder.

"We can use that donkey to haul our stuff too," he said. They tied their packs onto Cuddles, then started to move.

"Don't leave me," Ed called faintly. "Vultures . . . hyenas."

Moogar explained about the scavengers that would arrive shortly. Pretty stood over the old man, looking down at him.

"They got to live too, old man. I'd like to stay and watch that."

"Come on," said Moogar, barely concealing his hatred. "We got to move." Soon as I can, he thought, I got to get away from this crazy man.

"Okay," said Pretty. "Sorry we can't stay, old man." I'll watch the vultures and hyenas take care of Moogar, he thought. Moogar took the reins to lead the donkey. But Cuddles stood stubbornly, looking back at his master on the grass.

"Come, move," said Moogar, pulling the reins. Cuddles stood firm. Pretty kicked the animal hard with his heavy boot.

"Move, you------!" he shouted.

One more kick, and Cuddles began to move, looking back at Ed as she walked. They passed the tree bearing the good mark of the Phantom, pierced with bullet holes.

"I thought you said that was bad luck," said Pretty. "Call this bad luck? More supplies, and a donkey to carry our stuff?"

Moogar nodded without answering. Bad luck would come to this man. But he would be far away by that time.

The men and Cuddles were out of sight now. Ed tried to get up, but his wound hurt too much, and he was too weak. Maybe he could crawl. He tried that, moved a few feet, then collapsed. Now what? Couldn't just stay here. Maybe if he rested, he would gain some strength back, enough to reach the closest village. That would be the old folks' town, about a day's walk away. Not too far normally. But now? A few trails were closer. Hunters occasionally passed along them. If he could reach a trail, someone might find him in time. Rest now, he told himself. He was on his back, his hands shielding his eyes from the sun. A shadow passed over him, then another and another. He looked up in terror at the large silent wings that glided above him. Vultures.

Terrified, Ed began to crawl. If he could get under some bushes . . . but his strength failed. He collapsed once more, but as his hands clutched the grass he touched a stick. He grabbed it. A strong stick about five feet long. He knew the habits of vultures. As long as there was some life, some movement in him, they probably wouldn't attack. They preferred carrion. But on occasion, he'd seen them tear at fallen animals that were not yet dead.

A vulture flew low over him, its sharp claws almost touching his chest. A scout. Ed swung wildly at the bird. It landed a few feet away and watched. Three more vultures landed near the first. They were big birds, about four feet high, with long snakelike bare necks, beady yellow eyes, and long sharply curved beaks. They cackled and hissed, then began to moved toward him. He swung his stick again, lying on his side now.

"Get away from me, you varmints. You're not havin' lunch on me." The birds retreated a few feet. They knew wounded prey. It would struggle and resist for a time, growing weaker and weaker. Then, when movement became feeble, they would move in to tear the still living flesh with their cruel beaks. They would work fast, before their earthbound competition, the hyenas, moved in on the feast and chased them away. They advanced a step or two. Shielding his eyes from the bright sun with one hand so he could see them, he swung again. The birds stopped, but did not move back this time.

"This . . . is no way to go," he said aloud to the watching birds. "I've got a million friends . . . anyone would be glad . . . to help me . . . vamoose you varmints." He swung again, almost hitting the birds, they were that close. "Go away, you blasted . . ." he tried to shout, but his voice was barely above a whisper. He thrashed the stick in the air. It fell from his weak hand. He tried to wave his arms over his face as the birds closed in on all sides. One hovered a few feet above him, ready to land on his chest. The sharp talons brushed his shirt. He could see the great beak so near above him. He trembled with fear, and closed his eyes, helpless. This was it. He waited.

Then he heard a strange mixture of sounds, growling, hissing, cackling, a shot, the flapping of wings, then a deep soft voice.

"Ed, can you hear me?"

He opened his eyes and looked into the masked face of a stranger.

As the Phantom on Hero had neared this clearing, Devil suddenly stopped, ears alert.

"What is it, Devil?"

The wolf looked at his master, then raced through the bushes. The Phantom and Hero followed. In the clearing, they saw and heard a flock of vultures moving about and partially concealing the object of their attention. Devil raced at the flock, a growling roar coming from his open jaws. The awkward big birds ran flapping their wings, moving as fast as they could to escape from this attacker. Two didn't get away. Devil leaped, catching one by its snaky throat. The other one was settling on Ed's chest when the Phantom drew and fired. The big bird flapped its wings frantically once, then fell to the ground. The Phantom dismounted and rushed to the man. Though Ed had never seen him, the Phantom recognized the old trader, having seen him many times on the jungle trails.

The Phantom examined him quickly. He was wounded, but still alive. The cruel vulture beaks hadn't touched him. They'd come just in time. Devil finished the scavenger he'd attacked with one snap of his powerful jaws, then trotted over to his master to be rewarded with a pat. Hero, the mighty white stallion, stood like a marble statue, testing the air with his ears and nostrils. The Phantom opened Ed's shirt, and examined the bullet wound in the old man's abdomen. Ed's eyes were open. He tried to guess who the masked man was. He sighed.

"Thanks, stranger," he said finally, giving up. "Varmints were gettin' ready to have me for lunch. Will I be all right?"

"Bullet wound, close range. Doesn't look good. Who did it?"

"Pretty," said Ed. His voice was so low and weak the Phantom had to bend close to his lips to hear him. "Told those varmints, wouldn't like me. Too tough. Too sour." His voice sank to a mumble. He fainted.

Kneeling beside the unconscious man, the Phantom came to a quick decision. From his wide experience in treating the wounded, including himself, he knew Ed's wound was a bad one and that he shouldn't be moved with the bullet in him. For the Phantom to decide was to act. He quickly built a small fire, sterilized the sharp point of his hunting knife in the flames, wiped it with antiseptic from the kit in his saddle and cleansed the area around the wound. Then as Devil and Hero watched, he delicately and carefully probed for the bullet, found it, and removed it. He staunched the bleeding with antiseptic-soaked cotton, then bandaged it. He placed a mound of grass under Ed's head and covered him with Hero's saddle blanket. He built a small shelter of leaves to shelter Ed's face from the sun. Then as the white stallion grazed in the thick grass the man and wolf sat and watched their patient.

At twilight, Ed opened his eyes. He started to move. The Phantom's hand restrained him.

"Easy, Ed," he said. "You had a little operation."

"Water," croaked Ed.

The Phantom gave him a sip of sweet mountain water from his canteen.

"Operation?"

"Took out the bullet, Ed," said the Phantom. He held up the lead slug so Ed could see it. Ed grinned, then fell asleep for another hour. When he awoke, fireflies were flickering in the tall grass. '

"Took the bullet out of me?" he asked softly.

"It had to come out, so I could move you."

"You saved my life."

"It still needs more saving. I want to get you to Obano. They'll take you to Dr. Axel's hospital where you can get proper treatment."

"That Pretty shot me. He's a mean one. Then he robbed me. Took my wallet out of my pocket and took Cuddles."

"Cuddles?"

"My donkey."

The Phantom smiled in the firelight.

"Any idea where Pretty went? He and the other man?"

"The old folks' town. I heard them talkin'!"

"I'll have to move you now. It may hurt, Ed."

"Move away."

The Phantom picked up the old man and lifted him onto Hero's back. Ed leaned forward and put his arms around the stallion's neck. The Phantom tied his hands together so he wouldn't lose his hold. Then as the Phantom went over to stamp out the fire, Ed noticed the good mark on the tree. He smiled.

"I know who you are now," he said. "I've been in these parts a long time. I shoulda guessed right away."

"Save your breath, Ed. You've got a long ride back."

"I can take it," said Ed. "I'm as tough as an old rooster."

A full moon was shining through the trees as they moved out of the clearing. The old folks' town, thought the Phantom. I'll have to hurry to protect those helpless old people, from that human shark, Pretty, and the other one, Moogar. They had chosen well—a remote place, rarely visited by outsiders, unarmed, unable to resist such predators as those two. It was unfortunate he couldn't follow them now from here. They weren't too far ahead. But he couldn't leave Ed.

The old man needed medical attention. There was nothing else he could do, but take him back to Obano then return to the pursuit. Now, at least, he knew where to find them. But they might wreak terrible damage among the old folks before he could reach them.

"I've been in these parts more years than I remember," said Ed, mumbling through Hero's mane. "But I never thought I'd see you, much less have you save my life."

"Save your breath, Ed. You'll need it."

CHAPTER 17

A few miles to the east. Pretty and Moogar were stretched out on the grassy bank of a little stream. As was their arrangement, one slept while the other sat watch. It was Moogar's turn at watch. He sat against a tree trunk, his rifle over his knees, and looked at Pretty lying with his back to him. It would be easy to put a bullet in that back. But Moogar of Oogaan couldn't do that and Pretty of Brooklyn knew it They were only a few hours walk from the old folks' town now, and would reach there the next morning.

Ever since they'd left Killer's Town, he'd thought and planned how he would break off with this "mad dog" killer, and get away on his own. Now that they were in deep jungle, he no longer feared either police or Jungle Patrol. He could survive here. This was his home. His own tribe might even take him back. As for Pretty, he spoke none of the local languages, he had a total ignorance of the jungle, and despite his bullets would not last long. If he was ever going to make the break, Moogar told himself, now was the time. If he could get twenty yards away in this thick underbrush. Pretty could never find him. He listened to Pretty's breathing. He couldn't see the white face, but Pretty was motionless. Moogar got to his feet quietly and reached for a knapsack containing a few supplies, slipping it over his shoulder. One more glance at the recumbent Pretty, then he turned and, with rifle in hand, began to creep away.

"Going somewhere?" said the familiar voice.

Moogar whirled around, raising his rifle. But Pretty was pointing his gun at him.

"Drop it."

Moogar dropped his rifle. "What's the matter with you, you crazy?" he said, trying to bluff. "I was going-----"

"Going to relieve yourself?" said Pretty, mocking Moogar's delicate Oogaan expression and also seeming to read his mind, for this was exactly what Moogar was trying to say.

"I—er------" stammered Moogar.

"Bull!" said Pretty, getting up, his gun still in his hand. "You were trying to take off."

Moogar was ready to explode angrily, to admit he was leaving, to say he was a free man and that both should go their own way from here on. But he knew Pretty's temper. That gun in his hand could explode at any moment. He had seen too many die in front of Pretty—Koy, Matthew Crumb, Trader Ed. Die just like this, facing Pretty's wild smile and the barrel of his gun.

"You're not going anyplace," said Pretty. "I need you to get me out of this damn place."

Then they both knew that Pretty didn't want to shoot Moogar. At least, not yet. He needed him. But both also knew that if worse came to worst, he could shoot and would.

"Moogar," said Pretty in a mollifying tone of voice, "you been my pal. Know what I'm goin' to do for you? Do you, huh?"

Moogar shrugged.

"Those diamonds I brought—Koy only stashed some of them in his safe. I got the rest, most of them, buried outside that town. When the heat's off, we can go back and dig them up. Half for you. How about that?"

"Great," said Moogar.

Maybe Pretty thought Moogar believed the story. Moogar was sure it was a lie. No matter. If Pretty thought he believed him, then Pretty would be off guard and a second chance would come to get away. Pretty was holding Moogar's rifle.

"I'll keep this," he said flatly, offering no explanation. There was nothing Moogar could do about it. Maybe later. .. .

"Okay," said Moogar. He returned to his tree and started to sit down. "Now I sleep. You watch."

"No," said Pretty. "We're movin' now. Going to the old folks' place."

"Now? Travel at night?" Moogar was genuinely taken aback. No one in the jungle traveled at night.,

"Why not? It's cooler at night. You know the way."

"But you can't see as well at night. There are insects, snakes, holes."

"We got flashlights from the old geezer. We go," said Pretty firmly. His gun was still in his hand. He was taking no chances on being left alone in this crazy jungle. At the old folks' place, at least there were people. Maybe he could talk to some of them and wouldn't need Moogar any more. As Pretty held the gun, Moogar loaded Cuddles and they moved on, Pretty following the man and donkey taking no more chances.

The old folks' town was unique in the jungle. Unlike modern "civilized" races, the jungle folk had always respected the aged. As long as there was enough food, the young happily supported and cared for their elders. But in times of famine, a curious thing happened. The helpless among the aged were left in the jungle far from village walls to die of starvation or by the claw and fang of the jungle. But the unique factor is that the young did not force their aged into the jungles. The old people went of their own accord, following their ancient traditions whose origins were lost in antiquity. It was a simple, realistic decision. When there was not enough food to go around, the younger generations had the first right to survival. The aged had lived their lives; the young must be given their opportunity. This decision was made not by the young but by the Council of Elders in each jungle tribe. Often, the decision was made over the tearful protest of their children, grandchildren, and great-grandchildren. Once made, the decision was irrevocable. When the sad day arrived, the aged would move out through the gates for the last time, walking with canes or improvised crutches. Those too ill to walk would be carried on litters by the sturdier among them. This tragic exodus would be watched by the entire village from the walls. There would be weeping and wailing from the young as the aged proudly made their sacrifice for their children and walked to their deaths. This could occur anywhere along the tangled paths of the deep jungle. These events were remembered in songs, poetry, and stories that were handed down from generation to generation.

Such was the custom before the Phantom founded the old folks' town. (It had actually been the father of the present Phantom. But to the jungle, the Phantom was the Phantom.) When the old folks could no longer function or produce their share, they went of their own accord to the town. The tribes kept the town supplied with food and necessities. High walls protected them from animals. There was no need for protection against men. No one in the jungle would dream of molesting the town. It would be considered a sacrilege. In the town, the old folks lived a peaceful, secure life. They were happy with their peers and enjoyed this rest after a long, hard jungle life.

This is the idyllic place that Pretty and Moogar reached shortly after dawn. There was a mark on the gatepost. Neither noticed it at the time.

The high gates were closed to keep animals out. There was no lock, and it was a simple matter to open the latch.

They entered a small village with huts and larger communal buildings lining an immaculate street. A few old people were strolling at this early hour. Both men and women wore flowers in their hair, or in garlands about their necks, freshly plucked from the bushes that grew in profusion on all sides. They looked at the two men and the donkey and smiled gently. Travelers were rare here, but they passed by occasionally and, as in all deep jungle villages, received a night's hospitality. Pretty and Moogar walked on. In a courtyard, a dozen old people were seated at a long table having their breakfast. All turned and smiled. To Pretty, these wrinkled old blacks looked grotesque and alien. To Moogar, they appeared gentle and loving. Into this haven comes the killer, thought Moogar with a shudder. Memories of his brief days at missionary school returned. Were he and Pretty like two serpents entering the Garden of Eden? An old man approached them, smiling. Pretty watched him sharply, his hand on the butt of his gun.

"Welcome, young strangers," he said. "The hospitality of our village is yours. What are your needs?"

"What did he say?" demanded Pretty quickly. Moogar translated.

"Can't any of them talk English?"

Moogar snorted. "Are you kiddin'?" he said, using an expression he'd often heard Pretty use.

"We want hot water, soap. We want food, booze, and some clean beds," said Pretty to the old man. The old man looked at him inquiringly, then at Moogar. Pretty was suspicious. Maybe Moogar was holding out. It seemed impossible this old man couldn't understand a few simple words.

"Hot water . . . soap, food . . . booze . . . beds," he said loudly. Like many faced with someone who doesn't speak their language, he felt that if he shouted loudly enough, the man would understand. But the old man did not understand. He shook his head and waved his hands in confusion, looking appealingly at Moogar. This infuriated Pretty.

"We want a bath, food, booze you------!" he shouted, his face red. The old folks at the table and in the street stared.

"Pretty, he doesn't understand you," said Moogar, grinning.

This angered Pretty even more. "Tell him then," he shouted.

Moogar translated. The old man nodded, looking in fright at Pretty. Pretty slapped him hard, so that the old man staggered.

"And make it snappy!" he shouted. "Tell that to the dummy!" he shouted. Moogar translated.

Soon they were seated alone at the long table. The old people hurriedly piled it with food: fruit, nuts, and berries from the woods, wild and domestic fowl, baked fish. A feast. Again Pretty asked loudly for "booze." Moogar told him there were no alcoholic drinks in the place. He had to be satisfied with spring water or fruit juice. Pretty was satisfied. The heaps of food, the rapid service, and the obvious fear he inspired in all these old people pleased him.

"What a place," he said, stuffing breast of wild hen into his mouth. "A bunch of old crocks with nothing to do but wait on me. Bring me anything I want. I can live like a king here."

Good-humored for the moment, he nodded to Moogar who was also eating, and reached over to slap him on the back.

"I mean, we can live like kings. Right?"

After the feast, they walked around the village. Pretty looked into every hut. Word had spread about this violent young stranger. The old people looked at him with fright, their peaceful way of life shattered. Pretty was delighted with all he saw. So many old people, all potential servants, slaves to wait on him. As he made the tour, he formed a picture of the place. There was no opposition to him besides Moogar. And that would be solved soon. He could actually rule this place, live here like a king. It was a heady thought. All of his past life, all the misery—the hard experiences had prepared him, had toughened him so that he could take over here. He felt euphoric, like the time he'd loaded up on champagne with that fat blonde. Moogar had never seen him so happy and easy, though Pretty still carried the guns, his own and Moogar's. Then they passed the gatepost and saw the circular carving. It contained the good mark of the Phantom.

"That damn thing again. I didn't see that before. Did you put that there?"

Moogar snorted. "When would I have had time to do that?"

Pretty drew his pistol and fired at the mark. "Bad luck?" he said. "Brought us good luck before. How about that, you jungle bunnies," he said, looking at the crowd of old folks who were watching from a safe distance. They all reacted in fright at the gunshots. Deface the Phantom's mark? A terrible thing to do. What an evil man this one was, they whispered to each other.

"What are they yappin' about?" said Pretty.

Moogar shrugged. "They don't like the gun. They are afraid."

"They'll be more afraid before I'm through with them," he shouted, walking toward the small crowd. They parted quickly to let him pass. The people looked helplessly at Moogar.

"Do what he says. He is like the leopard. He kills for pleasure."

"Can you help us, Moogar of Oogaan?" asked the old spokeman.

"He took my guns. He is like a mad dog."

"He is not of this world [meaning the jungle]. How did he come here?"

Moogar had been afraid of this question. He answered, ashamed. "I brought him here. I am sorry for that. There is nothing I can do now. But the time will come."

"When he sleeps?" asked the old man wisely.

Moogar was confused. As an Oogaan, he could not kill in cold blood. Besides, his only hope was to get away from Pretty precisely when he was asleep. He glanced at the gatepost.

"He will come. He will help you," he said.

"Do you know his ways? How do you know he will help?"

"Because he always has," said an old woman, listening at the side. All smiled, relieved. Yes, he always had. There was hope in that. Their smiles faded as Pretty pounded the table and yelled.

"Moogar, what's going on over there?"

"They wanted to know how long we're stayin'. I told them I didn't know."

Pretty got his hot bath, a wooden tub of water heated over a campfire. He bathed alone in a hut with his guns within reach. He came out, refreshed, fed, bored. Nothing to drink. Nothing to do. The old people were gathered in little groups along the street, whispering. Should they send someone to the Llongo or Wambesi to get young warriors to help them? That meant a long trip through the dangerous jungle. None felt able to do this. Pretty sat at the long table watching them moodily, biting into a small fruit that looked like a plum but was sour. He threw it to the ground.

"Moogar, what are they jawin' about?"

"Nothing special," said Moogar.

Pretty was as impatient as a child and as easily bored. As he played with his gun on the table, he looked with disgust at the strange people and strange scene around him. How did he ever wind up here? All those old crocks watching, whispering. He had an idea. He grinned.

"Moogar, line up those old crocks. Have a race. A quarter mile race."

"You're crazy. That'd kill them."

"Don't use the word to me."

"Kill?"

"No. Crazy," snapped Pretty, memories of the mental hospital coming back to him. 'Tell them."

"Tell them yourself," said Moogar.

Pretty pointed his gun at Moogar. "You know I can't talk their talk. Do it."

Moogar walked to the groups and waved them together.

"He is trying to make you race. Go to your huts and stay there," he said. The old people understood. With scared glances toward Pretty they separated and started for their huts. "What are they doin'!" yelled Pretty.

"They don't want to race. Maybe you can talk them into it," said Moogar flatly. Pretty's temper flared. He raised his gun, but controlled himself. He needed Moogar in this strange world, needed him to talk to them. He looked about, saw something that pleased him, then barked at Moogar.

"Go to that post," he said. It was a thick upright used for tying up animals. "Tell those guys to come here with some rope."

The men obeyed, bringing not rope but a tough jungle vine. Pretty tested it with one hand, then ordered Moogar to sit against the post, with his arms behind him behind the post.

"Now tell them to tie you," said Pretty.

Moogar hesitated. Pretty fired a bullet into the post, a few inches above Moogar's head. The old men trembled at the sound. Seething with anger but helpless, Moogar ordered the old men to tie him. They obeyed. That done. Pretty went on one knee to test the tightness of the vine and the knots. Satisfied, he grinned at Moogar.

"That's where you sleep. Now I can sleep. I don't want you takin' off again, Moogar. I need you to talk to these monkeys."

He went to the nearest hut, chased an old woman out of it— she ran terrified down the street—then glared from the doorway.

"Tell these monkeys, if anybody tries to help you get loose, they'll be dead monkeys. Tell them!"

"He says he's going to sleep now," said Moogar. The old men nodded and went away. They didn't have to be told any more.

Pretty was tired, but before lying down, he carefully inspected the hut. A city boy, he had a terror of the big jungle bugs, particularly spiders, which were the size of saucers. But the place was immaculate. The old people were good housekeepers. He stretched out on the straw mat and dozed. Heavy sleep was not possible. He was still too nervous for that in this strange world where he understood not a word, where his only communication was with Moogar.

Outside, tied at the post, Moogar also slept out of sheer exhaustion. And from their windows and doorways, the old people watched and talked in whispers.

Sometime later, Moogar awoke with a start. Shadowy figures were bending over him. Old men with long knives that gleamed in the pale moonlight.

"You brought that monster here, Moogar of Oogaan," said the old spokesman.

"I did. I am ashamed," said Moogar, sweating with fear. "If I could be free, I know where I can find guns. I would return to destroy him." Even now he could not use the jungle word for "kill."

"Can we trust you, Moogar of Oogaan?"

"You have my sacred word by the blood of my ancestors," said Moogar. All the jungle knew the Oogaan worship of their ancestors. Such an oath was believed. The sharp knives sliced and hacked at the vine. It fell away from him.

"I will go and find guns."

"No, in that time, the mad dog will kill us. We will rush upon him now with knives." The spokesman handed him a long knife.

"No." said Moogar. "He will slaughter you like lambs. Wait until I return."

"We will not wait. He will slaughter some. But others will reach him with knives."

Moogar was on his knees, getting to his feet when Pretty's hut door burst open. Pretty stood in the doorway, a gun in each hand.

"I heard you gassin' out there. Don't know what you're sayin', but I don't have to be a genius to guess. You're makin' to take off, Moogar. I warned you."

Moogar dropped flat on the ground as Pretty's guns blazed. Two of the men closest to Moogar fell. The others rushed at Pretty with shrill cries, waving their knives. Pretty's guns blazed again. Two more fell. The others turned and fled. During the turmoil, Moogar crawled to the side, then got to his feet and ran. Pretty saw him in the moonlight running away. He aimed his gun. A dark figure, one of the fleeing old men, crossed his path. Furious, Pretty shot, missed, then chased after Moogar, who was disappearing in the darkness.

The big gates were closed for the night. Moogar did not stop to open the latch. He jumped high, reaching the points of the sharp stakes at the top of the wall, pulled himself up and swung over, dropping to the other side. His hands and legs were bleeding from deep scratches caused by the sharp stakes. But he ran like a frightened antelope, sweating and terrified. Pretty saw him go over the wall in the distance. He fired a shot, missed, then rushed to the gates. He opened the latch and flung open the gates. Beyond was the black jungle, unknown. No sign of Moogar. He was gone.

Pretty stood there, cursing with fury and growing fear. He was alone now in this alien place. As he turned back into the town, he saw the mark on the gatepost. The crossed sabers, or were they crossed P's? Bad luck? Phantom? What was all that malarkey. He closed the gate and fixed the latch. There were animals out there, big ones, lions. Maybe they'd get Moogar. He visualized that pleasant thought for a moment, then walked back warily, alone now.

In the dim shadows made by the pale moon, he saw the old people struggling to carry their wounded away. One pair saw him coming, dropped their burden, and ran away. He knew by now that they could not understand a single word of his, nor he of theirs. He needed some protection through the night while he slept. He must sleep, he told himself groggily, the days of exertion were catching up. If I can get a good night's sleep, then I'll go back the way we came, find that town again . . . what was its name . . . make somebody lead me to real people, he thought. He passed a hut where faint candlelight shone through an open window. He kicked open the door. An old man and old woman stared at him in fright, then hugged each other desperately. He looked about the hut. There was a coil of vine there, the kind they'd used to tie up Moogar. Pushing the old people into a corner and ignoring their whimpering, he tied them together. Then he pulled the lashed pair to the doorway, where other old people in the darkness could see them.

"If anybody bothers me, they'll get it," he shouted, pointing his gun at the old people. Then he shut the door and locked it with the inside latch. They can't understand English, but they'll understand that, he thought. He was right. They did. The old couple whimpered and uttered little cries as he came near them.

"Sit down," he said, pushing on their shoulders so that they sat on the dirt floor. He lay down on the straw mat. Now for some sleep. With daylight he'd decide what to do. Take off or stay. Play it by ear. See how it goes. He fell asleep, "with one eye open" as the jungle saying goes. This is how jungle animals sleep, alert at the slightest sound to awake and take off. Pretty was one of them, a predator living in constant danger between anger and fear.

Outside, the old people watched the hut from a distance. They understood the theory of hostages. If they attempted anything against the "mad dog" stranger, the old couple would be sacrificed. An uneasy calm settled over the old folks' town, the well-storied calm before the storm.

Moogar ran frantically for more than an hour without stopping. He tripped over roots and vines, picked himself up, ran again, as though pursued by demons, such was his fear of the malevolent Pretty. At length, exhausted and drenched with his own sweat, he stumbled into a clearing and leaned against a tree. He could run no farther. He had to rest. His legs were weak, his heart pounding, his breath coming in gasps. He put his arms around the tree to steady himself. His cheek rested against an unfamiliar surface, not bark. He stood back and stared. In the moonlight, he could see what it was. The carved good mark of the Phantom, the same one Pretty had shot at. He fingered the bullet holes.

Protection? Hadn't been much help to Old Ed or the people in the old folks town. Maybe Pretty was right. It didn't mean a thing. He realized that in his frantic run, he had covered the same distance it had taken them hours to cover the day before. And here he was back in the same place. He looked around for the old trader. No sign of him. Had the hyenas dragged him off? Most likely. He shuddered. He was feeling better now, secure in the thought that Pretty could never find him. Would he get guns, return to the old folks town? Maybe. Or get help from the tribes. He suddenly leaped in terror as something cold touched his ankle.

He recoiled at the sight of a big animal facing him—a wolf! Its nose had touched him. He had no weapons. He moved back slowly, feeling with his foot for a rock, something to protect himself against this big animal that stood staring at him.

Then a deep voice came from behind him. He stood stunned with surprise and fear.

"You are Moogar of Oogaan."

"I am."

"Turn around. Do not attempt to use a weapon."

"I . . . have no weapon," he said slowly as he turned, not knowing what he would see or expected to see.

What he did see was probably the last thing he might have imagined. A huge white stallion—and seated on its broad back a big powerful figure, hooded and masked. Moogar had never seen him before. But from the years of tales and legends, he knew who he was, who he must be. He leaned back against the tree that bore the mark. Strong men do not faint easily, even when they are exhausted. But for the moment, Moogar almost slipped into unconsciousness, such was the shock of the moment.

The sight of the Phantom on a dark jungle night can freeze the blood—old jungle saying.

CHAPTER 18

"Where is Pretty?"

The figure on the horse knew about Pretty. It had always been said that he knew about everything.

"In the old folks' town."

"Why did you take that killer to those poor old people? He will frighten them, if not worse," said the deep voice out of the darkness. It was already worse as he would find out.

"Before I knew him well, I made the mistake of telling him about the town. He took my guns. He made me take him there," said Moogar in a sudden rush of words.

"The Jungle Patrol wants both of you. You will wait at this tree until I return." A small object came through the air from the shadowy figure and fell at Moogar's feet. It was a short knife and matches tied together. "You are a jungle man. With these, you can manage for yourself. Do not run away. If I have to go after you, it will be bad for you. Do you understand?"

Moogar nodded and stammered his agreement. The last thing he wanted now was to have this big figure come out of the dark after him.

"I will wait here. I promise," said Moogar as he stooped to pick up the knife and matches. There was a slight swish in the grass and leaves. When he looked up, horse and rider and wolf were gone.

Moogar stared with amazement into the darkness, then listened keenly. Were those hoofbeats in the soft loam, heard for a moment, then gone? *The Phantom moves on cats' feet* was another old jungle saying. Was it true about his celebrated stallion as well? Moogar was thankful he had escaped from the old folks' town, glad this grim figure wasn't coming after him. He felt no pity for Pretty. The killer had it coming to him.

Moogar was suddenly alarmed. Pretty was heavily armed and would shoot at every shadow. Was it true what the legends said that the Ghost Who Walks was the Man Who Cannot Die? Though stem and ominous, that shadowy figure on the white stallion nevertheless sounded like a real man.

"Pretty has guns. He will shoot," he shouted. There was no answer except for the chirping of crickets in the grass and the shrill piping of tree frogs. He felt foolish, shouting in the darkness like that. As for his own future, that was too much to face or think about. All he could do was wait as he had been told. He sank to the base of the tree, the knife in his hand. He would sleep, and if the big cats came, then they would come. He was tired of fighting.

The Phantom reached the walls of the old folks' town shortly before dawn. He left Devil with Hero, hidden in nearby bushes. As Moogar had done, he made a running leap to grasp the tops of the sharp stakes on the wall. But he knew about the stakes and avoided the points. He swung easily over the fence and dropped lightly to the ground. The moon was behind a cloud and he moved on in the darkness.

Most of the old people were awake in their huts, staring at each other or whispering. In one hut, they nursed the wounded. Luckily, Pretty's wild shots had killed no one outright. But several were in serious condition, requiring attention the town could not offer. In another hut, several of the elderly leaders sat together around the feeble light of a single candle, trying to decide what to do about the killer. Had Moogar escaped or been killed in the woods? None knew. If he had escaped, would he return with guns or with help? Who could tell? And what of the Phantom? His good mark, promising protection, was on their gatepost. He himself had personally visited the town many years before. None presently living there had seen him, but the tale of his visit had been retold many times. (That the visitor was the Phantom's father would have meant nothing to them. The Phantom was the Phantom.)

"Perhaps we hope foolishly for the Phantom. How can he know about us?" asked an oldster of Wambesi.

"The Phantom knows all," said the old man of Llongo next to him.

"If that is so, why did he permit this killer to come here?"

The old men sighed.

"The Phantom will not come. Either he does not know of this or if he knows he has deserted us," said an old man of Morf the fisher folk.

That was undeniable logic and all sighed and fell into depressed silence. It was at that moment that the Phantom slipped into the doorway, almost without a sound. The old men gasped.

"Shh," he warned them. "I have come to help you."

None needed to be told who he was. His huge figure seemed to fill the hut. To these frail old men, he was a giant.

"Where is the white?" he said.

They pointed to the hut, and explained about the two hostages tied in there.

"He will kill them if anyone tries to enter. We are sure of that," said the elder spokesman. "We have seen him. He kills without care. He is a man with no soul."

"He has a demon for a soul," corrected the old man of Mori. All nodded. That explained heedless killers like Pretty. All the old men had known one or more like that in their lifetimes.

A demon for a soul thought the Phantom. A perfect description of what other old men in white coats and glasses would call by a fancier name—paranoid, schizophrenic. These old men who lived close to the earth knew. A demon for a soul.

"Stay in here. I will go for him," said the Phantom and he slipped out into the darkness as quietly as he had come. The old men looked at each other with jubilation. He had come. He knew and he had not deserted them. But their happiness was tinged with fear. For most of them, it was the first view of the Phantom. And though he was big and powerful, he appeared to be flesh and blood as other men. And the mad dog's bullets could kill that flesh as well as theirs. Or was he—the Man Who Cannot Die?

The Phantom moved silently over the soft ground to the hut. He crouched at the thin wall and listened. There were slight stirrings inside, faint murmurs. Pretty was evidently awake or dreaming, talking to himself or talking in his sleep. The Phantom was half-right on both counts. Pretty was half-asleep, coming in and out of tortured dreams, muttering to himself. The old couple, unable to sleep, sat lashed together in the corner, watching their captor with terrified eyes. The Phantom considered. The windows and door were closed, latched with crossbars inside. He could break through the walls or door quickly, but not quickly enough to keep Pretty from shooting the two hostages. He guessed correctly that Pretty either sat or was lying down with his gun in his hand. Dawn was breaking over the tree-tops. He must move now. He knelt below the window and whispered loudly.

"Pretty, Pretty."

He strained his ears, and was on his knees now. He looked at the old folks. They were watching him with such terror, he didn't know if they had heard anything and couldn't ask them.

"Pretty, Pretty."

The sound had been near the window. Now it came from the door, then from the other window across the room. Only Moogar knew his name. Had he come back? Possible. The voice was louder now.

"Pretty, Pretty."

That wasn't Moogar's voice. He got up and began to move in the direction the sound came from, hoping to hear footsteps. He heard nothing. Silence, then the loud whisper from the other side. He rushed to that side. The whisper came from another side. Pretty turned to the old couple.

"Do you hear that? Answer me you old------!"

They huddled against each other, not knowing what was coming. He watched them closely to see if their eyes moved in the direction of the whispers. But they didn't. The old people continued to stare at him with their eyes fixed with fear. They were so frightened by this violent stranger, it's possible they heard nothing.

"Pretty, Pretty."

This time from the door. He rushed to it and pounded the wood with the butt of his gun.

"Stop it!" he shouted. "This is a trick to get me out. It won't work."

"Pretty, Pretty."

He fired two shots through the door. The explosions reassured him. Through the old folks' town, the people trembled at the sound. Had he shot the hostages? Pretty listened. Had his shots hit?

"Pretty, Pretty."

This time high up, from the edge of the ceiling where it touched the walk He shot again, three times, into the roof.

"Pretty, Pretty."

His patience was exhausted. His nerves were frayed, at the breaking point.

"Get up you two!" he shouted at the old couple. They stared, naturally not understanding. Angrily, he grabbed them by their thin arms and jerked them to their feet, then shoved them towards the door. They trembled and whimpered, certain that he would kill them now. Daylight was coming through the cracks of the door and window and openings in the ceiling and walls. He threw off the latch bar and pulled the door open. His gun was pointed against the old woman's head.

"Listen," he shouted. "Whoever is out there. I'm standing here with my gun at this old dame's head. Whoever you are, if you have any guns, drop them where I can see them. Then show yourself. Do this by the time I count three or I swear I will blow off the top of this old dame's head. I will say all this once more, then start counting."

The old woman felt the cold steel barrel against her temple. She began to scream, then collapsed to the floor, dragging her lashed partner with her. Pretty followed them down to the floor, kneeling beside them, his gun still held at her head. In response to the screams, the sound of wailing came from the village. Pretty repeated his instructions, shouting them through the open doorway, then began to count.

"One . . . two . . ."

A gun dropped in front of the doorway, then a second gun, tossed from the side. Pretty did not move, his eyes glaring, sweat pouring from his face.

"Show yourself," he yelled.

A huge figure stepped into the doorway, blotting out the early morning light. Pretty stared. Hooded, masked, a weird skin-tight outfit like—like something.

"I've dropped my guns," said the man in a deep voice. "Take yours away from that woman's head."

Pretty almost breathed a sigh of relief. In this alien nightmare world, here at least was a man who spoke his language. He stood up, his gun pointed at the stranger's broad chest.

"Back, up slow like," he ordered. The stranger obeyed and Pretty followed him outside the hut. In the daylight he stared curiously at his captive. Pretty was still trembling from his recent ordeal, but the sounds of his own language had restored his confidence. This man was big, like a professional football player or a heavyweight boxer. His eyes were masked in some way that concealed his eyes. There was a large death's head on his broad leather belt, a ring on a finger of each hand.

"Who in hell are you?" he asked.

The masked man stood quietly and said nothing.

"I heard you talk. You said my name. You heard what I asked you. Who are you?"

"Men call me by many names," said the deep voice. "Some call me the Phantom."

This was a jolt for Pretty. He almost dropped his gun.

This was the one Moogar kept talking about. The one . . . he looked again at the death's head on the belt. It all began to come together.

"You were at Killer's Town. Are you the one who did all that? Blew up the warehouse, made all those skull marks like that?"

"I was there," said the deep voice.

Pretty noticed that though his gun was pointed at the broad

chest, the stranger stood relaxed and easy, showing no fear.

"And you knocked out all those guys and made off with that redhead? Hey, what did you do with that little dish?"

"Home with her father."

"Took her home? Aren't you the fool?" said Pretty.

The stranger did not reply. He seemed to stand motionless, like a statue, showing no sign of even breathing.

"How did you know I was here. How did you know my name?"

"Everyone knows your name. You are well known in these parts," said the stranger.

Pretty motioned to a bench. "Sit down there," he commanded. The stranger obeyed. Pretty sat on a beneh facing him, but the gun remained aimed at him.

"I can kill you, you know." said Pretty.

"You won't. I'm your only hope of getting out of here."

"You going to get me out?"

"That's why I came."

Pretty could hardly believe his ears. This stranger was so cool, so calm. What did he mean?

"You came here to help me?"

"To get you out of the jungle."

Pretty considered. That could mean anything.

"I want to get out of here," he said suddenly. "I want to go where there are real people."

"Aren't these real people?"

"These monkeys?"

The stranger remained silent. It was upsetting, having this big man sitting there and not being able to see his eyes. "Why do you wear all that?" said Pretty.

The stranger shrugged.

"When I ask questions, I want answers," said Pretty, flaring up.

The stranger sat quietly. Pretty realized he couldn't handle the man this way. Both knew Pretty needed him.

"Who are you anyway?"

"I told you."

"Phantom? Means nothing. Not good enough."

"Then, let's just say I'm a masked man."

Pretty grinned. He was beginning to see the light.

"Oh, a hood, a jungle hood."

The stranger smiled.

"Look, we can make a deal," said Pretty eagerly.

"Why not untie those people first?"

"Why not? You do it, Mr. Spook."

Pretty laughed appreciatively at his own humor. The masked man moved to the old couple and untied them. They were stiff and exhausted from their ordeal.

"You had a bad time," he told them. "Go to another hut now and sleep."

They nodded, too weary to thank him. They staggered off, hand in hand.

"What did you say to them?"

"I told them to sleep."

"Do they think you're the spook?" said Pretty, laughing again.

In the huts, the old people watched. They saw the Phantom sitting with the killer. They heard the laughter. What could this mean? Was the Phantom making friends with this mad dog? That seemed impossible. Was he afraid of the gun and agreeing to join the outlaw? What did it mean? So they whispered among themselves, knowing the Phantom was their last hope. This killer could move among them like a plague, destroying all of them. How could the Phantom sit in such a friendly manner with this terrible man from outside? Were they really friends? That could not be, they argued. "Yet," said the logician among them, the oldster of the Mori, the fisher folk, "they are sitting as friends and making jokes and discussing matters. The real Phantom could not do that with such a man. So it follows, this is not the real Phantom but an imposter." They all gasped at the thought, and their hopes died. Instead of one terror, would there now be two? The mad dog and an imposter?

"Man, you've really got this crowd spooked," said Pretty, laughing. "How do you do it?"

The masked man shrugged.

"Whatever it is, you got them all scared dizzy. The way you handled that thing at Koy's place. Wow. Did you do that all alone?"

The masked man nodded. He was watching Pretty carefully. The killer was becoming chatty and casual, and the gun was gradually lowering in his hand. Then Pretty suddenly stiffened, his face grim, the gun pointed at the broad chest.

"Wait a minute," he said. "When you did all that, the Jungle Patrol, the fuzz, were all waiting outside. You were working with them!"

"I work alone."

"Yeah," said Pretty, Ms eyes now flickering with the wild light. "What were you doing when they grabbed all those guys?"

"I opened Koy's safe."

Pretty stared at him with open admiration, almost hero worship. Nothing that the Phantom could have said would have impressed him as much. Safecrackers are the aristocrats of the underworld, at the top of the pecking order. "You saw all the stuff? My diamonds and all the rest?" The Phantom nodded.

"Wow! Where is it now?"

The Phantom smiled briefly, but did not answer.

"But you know?"

The Phantom nodded.

"Look, we gotta deal?" said Pretty excitedly. "You'll take me out of this place, back to a real place, real people?" The Phantom nodded. Pretty smiled, his mind going a mile a minute. Once out of the jungle, he could force this hood to show him the cache. All the stuff in Koy's safe. Wow! Not only the diamonds he and Finger had brought, but the rest he'd heard about—gold from the bank robbery, gems and drugs from Hong Kong, diamonds from London, another heist from Amsterdam, and probably lots more he didn't know about. All in Koy's safe. Now this guy had it and it would be his, Pretty's, for the taking. All it would take would be one bullet above that mask, he thought, as he smiled at the Phantom.

"Time to go," said the Phantom, standing up.

"Right," said Pretty eagerly. The Phantom's guns were still on the ground. "I'll keep those for a while," said Pretty casually, his own gun barrel still pointed at the Phantom.

"You don't trust me with them?"

"I don't trust anybody," said Pretty. "Maybe later. Don't worry. I can handle anything that comes along."

"I know."

"What do you mean by that?" said Pretty, as always, touchy as a boil.

"I've heard you're a great shot."

Pretty smiled. It was rare that he received compliments for anything. "That's no lie," he said, almost modestly.

Then, suddenly suspicious, gun pointed: "Who told you that, Moogar?"

"Who?"

"Never mind." How would this creep know? "You're damn right I can shoot. I never miss. Don't forget that."

"I won't," said the masked man casually. "I'll bet you can't hit that bird up there."

"Yeah? What bird?" said Pretty, unable to refuse a challenge. It was one of the oldest tricks in existence, but Pretty fell for it. He looked up into the sky over his shoulder where the masked man had indicated. It was the last view he would have of this jungle, or any jungle. For as his head turned ever so slightly, his eyes no longer watching the Phantom, a steel fist crashed upon his jaw. The sound of that blow made the old people wince for a hundred yards around. Pretty dropped like a rock, in a heap. Those who were watching said the Phantom's arm moved faster than the eye could see.

Phantom moves like lightning in the sky—old jungle saying.

CHAPTER 19

The old people poured out of their huts and ran toward the Phantom from all directions, as he stood without moving, looking at the fallen man. The old people chanted and laughed and cried as they ran or walked or hobbled. This was no imposter. This was their friend whose sign had promised protection, and who had kept his promise.

"Ghost Who Walks . . . Ghost Who Walks," they chanted in their many tongues . . . for the tribal dialects differ. Then they surrounded him, touching him, patting him, kissing his hands, their happy frail voices sounding like a chorus of forest birds. He put his powerful arms around those closest to him to reassure them. He knew the torment and fear they had endured. Then they stood back as their spokesman, the elder of Wambesi, addressed him.

"That was a terrible blow. Is he dead?"

"No," said the Phantom. "I was tempted. This is a hateful killer. But at the last moment, I held back."

"Held back?" said the elder, marveling. "He is unconscious. I believe he has broken bones. And if you had not held back?"

"He might be dead."

The oldsters discussed this softly among themselves, then quieted as the elder spoke again.

"May I ask another question, O Ghost Who Walks?"

The Phantom nodded.

"I observed while he was in the hut with Nagy and Dryga [the old hostages], the door was open and you were at the side. You had the opportunity to shoot him in the back. You did not. Why?"

"I cannot shoot any man in the back, even one such as this. To do that would be to decide his fate. That was not for me to do."

All nodded and understood, for all jungle folk know that the fates of all men everywhere are spun by the three-headed Witch of Grimgaldny, within whose six hands the life strands of all mankind are interwoven.

"He grieviously wounded two of our people," said the elder.

"I will send warriors with litters to bear them to a place of healing," said the Phantom.

The elder of Wambesi, a famous warrior in his time, drew his long knife from his woven belt.

"Should we not judge this evil man here?"

"No, man of Wambesi. He caused your people harm, yet he killed two men or more in a faraway town. And they will judge him for his murders."

The talk was over. The Phantom draped Pretty over the back of Cuddles. Trader Ed's patient donkey had been tethered nearby all this while. He lashed the unconscious man on the pack saddle, so that his head and arms hung down one side, his legs down the other. Then the Phantom opened the big gates and whistled, a loud clear sound. In a few moments, a big white stallion bounded to the gates. At his side was the large gray mountain wolf. All the oldsters knew these famous animals by reputation, the Phantom's Hero, the Phantom's Devil.

He placed the end of Cuddle's lead rope in Devil's mouth, then swung up into the saddle of the great stallion. Hero reared high into the air, the Phantom waved, and they started off, Devil leading the donkey with its burden—Pretty. All the people of the old folks' town rushed to the gates and waved until they were out of sight Then they closed the gates and went back to their tables or huts. They would discuss these two dramatic days for months and years to come. And as time passed, the legend would grow as legends do. And the figures would grow as well, until the Phantom and Pretty would tower above the treetops: the good giant versus the evil giant And the blow that felled the evil giant would topple high trees and crack the very earth. Yes, there was plenty to talk about for a long time. But once more, all was well in this peaceful haven of the old people.

When the Phantom reached the clearing, Moogar was waiting, seated at the foot of the tree that bore the good mark. He jumped to his feet and ran to them.

"Is he dead?" he said, looking at the dangling Pretty.

"No. A few fractures. He can be patched up."

"What—what happened to Trader Ed?"

"He would be at Dr. Axel's hospital by now."

Moogar sighed with relief.

"I didn't shoot him," he said.

"I know. You didn't run away."

"I'm tired of running away. I want to go back, take my punishment, get it over."

"A good decision, Moogar. When you are free, go back to your people of Oogann. They need good men."

"Good men?" said Moogar bitterly. "I'm a criminal. I'll be an ex-con. Such are not welcome."

"True. Your people will be suspicious. They have a right to be. You made them so. But you must earn your welcome. I know you to be a man of good heart. They must learn that, too."

Dawn at the front gates of Jungle Patrol headquarters. The night guards stumbled sleepily back to their bunks. The yawning day guards took their stations. Then the Sergeant- in-Charge noticed two pair of feet sticking out from bushes on the drive just outside the gates. One pair of feet was bare and black. The other pair was booted and, on further inspection, turned out to be white. The owner of the white feet was unconscious, his jaw wrapped in a bandage. The owner of the black feet was propped up on his elbow, waiting for them.

"I'm Moogar. This is Pretty. You've been looking for us."

The arrival of these two, the last missing fugitives from the notorious Killer's Town, was a mild sensation. No one ever knew how they really got there. A few had a good idea. Moogar, the petty criminal, had given himself up. But Pretty, the "mad dog" killer, was in no state to give himself up. He was in the hospital for two weeks before he could talk. When he could, he refused to answer any questions. In his own mind, he was not certain how it happened. He remembered looking for the bird. Then a smashing pain and blackout. How long ago had that been? Over two weeks? Wow!

As he regained his strength, he talked to a black lawyer provided by the court. America was trying to extradite him for the killings at the Jewelry Mart "Can they get me?" he asked.

"Bangalla has no extradition treaty with your country."

"That means they can't get me. Good."

"No. You will be tried here."

"For what?"

"The murder of Matthew Crumb."

"Who? Oh, that old guy. I didn't do it."

"They have eyewitnesses. Also verbal reports of Crumb's last words, accusing you."

"Uh, what are my chances?"

"Not good."

"What'll happen to me? Life?"

"We are an old-fashioned nation. We still have capital punishment. Execution by hanging."

Pretty sat up in bed, his hands to his throat.

"No," he said. "No! Let them—what do you call it—extradite me."

"In America, you killed an old night watchman and a police officer."

"Sure. But I'll get off. I got a mental history. You know —mental history? That means they send me to the bug-house."

"Bughouse?"

"Foolish factory, insane asylum, stupid! Know what happens then? Two years, three years, they give me a review. They let me out, cured."

"Is that possible for a man like you?" said the black lawyer, genuinely shocked.

"All the time." Pretty grinned. "So extradite me, Uncle Sam." It's going to be all right, he thought. I'll beat this, like I've always beaten everything. I'll come back, find that Moogar who was ready to bear witness against me, then find that masked guy, shoot first, enough to drop him, find out where he hid that stuff. It's going to be all right "I'll beat this," he told the black lawyer.

"No. You will not be sent back to America. You will be tried here. The court has decided."

"I'll be sent to a nut—to a mental place?"

"We have none here; the mentally sick stay in the villages."

"I got no village to stay in," said Pretty anxiously.

"Correct. Also, you are a murderer. No village would be safe with you in it."

"Wait a minute, are you my lawyer?"

"I have been assigned. You will receive a fair trial."

"Okay. But tell me . . . my lawyer . . . how will it come out?"

"We are an old-fashioned country, as I have said. You will be hanged by the neck until you are dead."

And that is what happened. Moogar received a three-year sentence with time off for good behavior.

The former pesthole, Killer's Town, was a busy place now as Dr. Axel's Coast Hospital. The casino and bar had become modern clinics with the latest equipment, most of it contributed by grateful donors of many lands whose stolen goods had been returned from Killer's Town. It was no longer a forbidden place. Traffic flowed through the jungle to this place, patients and visitors. The gates were no longer closed—and on the gate post was the familiar sign of crossed sabers . . . or were they crossed P's—the good mark of the Phantom.

Colonel Weeks sat in his office with Sandy, Tamos, Hill, and Morgan.

"Colonel, that place. Killer's Town—who broke it up?" said Hill.

"When we got in there, we found these skull marks painted all over the place. Some kind of voodoo? Who did that?" said Morgan.

"Who brought in Trader Ed after that creep shot him?" said Sandy.

"Maybe it's the same one who brought in Moogar and that 'creep,' as you call him." said Weeks.

"And who would that be?" said the four patrolmen, almost in unison.

Weeks was doodling with a pen on a scrap of paper—curious designs—a mask—a skull—and something that looked like crossed sabers—or crossed P's.

"Who? That is the question. Perhaps you'll know someday. Excuse me now, gentlemen. I've work to do."

Colonel Weeks knew. Dr. Axel knew. Moogar and Traded Ed knew. The old folks' town knew. To the rest it would remain a mystery.

The killer was gone. The jungle breathed a sigh of relief.

A Sneak Peak at Volume 10:
The Goggle-Eyed Pirates!

S he didn't suspect anything.
    The darkening waters of the Atlantic stretched calmly in
every direction, a luxurious peacefulness was settling down on
the Lido Deck of the S.S. Paradiso as twilight approached. Only a
single swimmer remained at the deck pool. The board thwacked
as the man made a final dive.

    Diana Palmer sat alone at a round plastic-topped table in
the Lido Cocktail Lounge, sipping absently at her one gin and
tonic of the afternoon. A slim, pretty, dark-haired girl, she was
looking through the full-length blue-tinted window, not at the
swimming pool but at the ocean beyond.

    Mawitaan is over in that direction, she thought to herself.
We should see her fights in a few hours.

    Mawitaan, the next stop for this cruise finer, was a large
port town and the capital of Bangalla.

    A blender began to whir behind the bar. The pudgy pink-
faced man who was leaning on the bar, said, chuckling, "So that's
how you make one of those drinks, huh?"

    I hope he'll be able to meet me, Diana thought. Well, let's
keep our fingers crossed.

    The only other people in the lounge were a young Dutch
couple, newlyweds, very blond and tanned. The girl sat watching
her husband, stirring her drink without looking down at it. On
her wrist was a large diamond bracelet. As the soft orange lights

came on, the circle of bright stones flashed for an instant.

"Hey, now, that tastes good, great!" exclaimed the pudgy, pink man at the bar. "You ought to come back to Detroit, Michigan, and teach the bartenders at the Sheraton-Cadillac Hotel a few tricks." He took another slurping sip. "What's your name, anyhow?"

"Peter, sir," replied the mustached bartender.

"Peter what?"

"Maresca, Peter Maresca, sir."

"Glad to know you, Pete . . . is that what they call you, Pete?"

"No, sir. Peter."

"Okay, then, Peter. My name is Harlan Brupp. Kind of a funny name, I admit, but I guess I'm stuck with it."

Placing her glass on the table, Diana gathered up her handbag and scarf and left the room.

Night was closing in. The water already seemed black, the spray of the liner's wake a pale gray.

Diana stood at the rail for several minutes. She had her eyes narrowed, trying to spot the first lights of Mawitaan. "Too soon, I guess," she said to herself. "I know he'll be there. He said he would, unless something urgent came up."

She turned away from the rail, found the stairwell, and climbed down the metal steps. Her cabin was two levels down, on the boat deck. Aboard the S.S. Paradiso that was called the Dante Deck, each deck being named after an eminent Italian. Of course, Diana reflected as she descended, in his life a good many emergencies do come up, but. . . no. I'm sure he'll be there to meet me.

Diana's cabin, T-43, was an outside one on the port side. As she neared the door of the room, the door of T-51 opened.

Out stepped Brian Folkestone, a long, lean young man. "Good evening, Miss Palmer," he said, grinning. He had a pleasant outdoor face and sandy hair worn relatively short.

"Looking forward to Mawitaan?" she asked, inserting her key.

"Not especially, no," he replied. "Frankly, the part of these ocean cruises I like best is when you are out in the middle of the vast unlimited sea with nothing at all about. You know, something of that 'water, water, everywhere' feeling." He grinned again. "Of course, when one has had the unfortunate privilege of growing up in Liverpool, one can never think completely kindly thoughts about any harbor town."

"Coming from the Midwestern United States," said Diana, "I'm still not jaded, I guess. And besides. . ." She let the sentence trail off unfinished.

"Besides you're meeting someone important to you in Mawitaan," the blond young man finished for her.

"How'd you know that?"

His grin flashed wider. "Just another sample of the fabled Folkestone perceptiveness, Miss Palmer. You have a look about you indicating you're going to be met. And I've noticed during the day that whenever Mawitaan was mentioned, you got a special sort of look in your eyes."

"I didn't realize I was so obvious."

"Only to someone with the fabled Folkestone perception," he said. "Would you allow me to have a drink with you. Miss Palmer? It's probably my last chance."

"Thanks, but I'm just coming back from one of the cocktail lounges," said the dark-haired girl. "And I have some things to take care of before dinner. But perhaps after dinner and before we dock?"

After a second, Folkestone said, "Yes, let's do that. I'll find you then." Giving her a final grin, he went striding off down the pale-blue corridor.

Diana's nose wrinkled slightly as she pushed open the door of her cabin. A faint scent lingered in the corridor, a mingling of lemon and sandalwood. The aftershave Folkestone always wore.

"He's a little generous with it, maybe," Diana mumbled to herself. She closed the door, crossed to the square porthole, and looked into the night.

Still no sign of the shore lights of Mawitaan.

Peter, the Lido Deck bartender, went walking down the corridor which led from the rear of the lounge to the radio room. On his upturned palm rested a tray which held a can of cola and a plastic glass full of shaved ice. He knocked on the door of the communications room, humming under his breath.

"Yo," called out a voice inside.

Peter pushed into the room. "I don't see how you can drink this stuff night after night."

The redheaded, freckled radioman was sitting in a squeaky swivel chair in front of his equipment. "Hard liquor makes me dizzy." He grabbed the can off the tray and yanked the opening tab.

Peter handed him the glass, swung the now empty tray up under his arm. He leaned against a pale-blue wall. "Some guy told me this afternoon I'd like it in the United States."

"Didn't you inform him you hailed from Newark?"

Peter shrugged. "People expect something more romantic than that on a cruise. I told him I lived in Milan."

The door swung suddenly open. "Surprise," announced a fluty falsetto voice.

The two men turned toward the door.

A tall figure in a long tan caftan stood there. He held a .38 revolver in his gloved right hand. A stocking mask had been pulled over his head, a mask with a wide toothy grin painted on it. Covering his eyes were a pair of thick goggles.

"What is this?" asked the radioman, the soft drink can still bubbling in his hand.

"What the hell do you think it is?" asked the goggle-eyed figure. "It's piracy on the high seas, lads."

After ordering'both of them over against the far wall, the figure proceeded to smash the radio-sending equipment with a crowbar he'd brought along for the purpose.

COMING SOON FROM HERMES PRESS

Volume 10: The Goggle-Eyed Pirates!